Penguin Books

a

stranger

here

Gillian Bouras was born in Melbourne in 1945. She worked as a teacher in Australia before moving to Greece with her husband and children in 1980. Her first book about this experience was *A Foreign Wife*, published in 1986, and this was followed by *A Fair Exchange* in 1991. *Aphrodite and the Others*, published in 1994, won a New South Wales State Literary Award in the same year, and in 1995 was shortlisted for the prestigious UK Fawcett Book Prize.

GILLIAN BOURAS

a
stranger
here

Penguin Books

Penguin Books Australia Ltd
487 Maroondah Highway, PO Box 257
Ringwood, Victoria 3134, Australia
Penguin Books Ltd
Harmondsworth, Middlesex, England
Viking Penguin, A Division of Penguin Books USA Inc
375 Hudson Street, New York, New York 10014, USA
Penguin Books Canada Limited
10 Alcorn Avenue, Toronto, Ontario, Canada M4V 3B2
Penguin Books (NZ) Ltd
182–190 Wairau Road, Auckland 10, New Zealand

First published by Penguin Books Australia 1996

10 9 8 7 6 5 4 3 2 1

Typeset in 11.5pt/16pt Weiss by Post Typesetters
Printed in Australia by Australian Print Group

National Library of Australia
Cataloguing-in-Publication data:

Bouras, Gillian, 1945– .
    A stranger here.
    ISBN 0 14 026114 1.
    1. Bouras, Gillian, 1945– Fiction. I. Title.
A 823.3

Acknowledgements

I wish to thank Meriel Wilmot-Wright, without whose friendship and good cooking this book would not have been written.

Many thanks also go to two hospitable people who have the same initials: M.S.

It is impossible to estimate the debt I owe Dr G. M. Dow, my mentor and friend, who has given freely of great affection, support and guidance for over twenty years.

The author is grateful for the assistance of a one-year Writer's Fellowship from the Literature Board of the Australia Council. The quote on page 27 from Sylvia Plath's poem 'Morning Song' is published in *Ariel* by Faber & Faber Ltd, London. Paul Scott's *Staying On*, quoted on page 44, is published by Longman, London.

In memory of my mother.

For her grandsons.

And for LBB, who redrew stubborn lines into a triangle, and showed me how to make a warm blanket out of the warp and weft of horizontal and vertical affections.

Childhood has no forebodings; but then
it is soothed by no memories
of outlived sorrow.

George Eliot

This is a story of three women.

The first, Artemis, is a Greek village woman who has a family, as have most village women. She did not marry young by the standards of her time, for her father loved her very much and took considerable trouble over the matter of a husband. The woman did not complain about this prescribed patience, for it was her business to obey and obedience brought its reward. Eventually she married a priest, and together they had four daughters and three sons, children to be proud of.

Their first child, a son and the most handsome of all the children, proved unexpectedly adventurous. At the start, it has to be admitted, the adventure was forced on him – someone had to earn dowry money for all those daughters – but in her heart Artemis felt that no good would come of his going to foreign parts. Being different, changing the pattern, brought down God's wrath. Always. One of her brothers had gone to war and died, another to America where he disappeared. Forever. Still the money was needed, so the son went. He did not disappear; he came back. But not alone.

Now his mother, an old woman, sits and sits and does nothing else. Nobody understands that she still sees, hears, understands and *knows*. Not as regularly as she would like, for she often finds it hard to pick up and grasp the thread of meaning. This is the way things are in old age; she realises this. But she takes in a great deal, and finally she has the chance to process what she takes in. She has never had this chance before: hers has been a lifetime of very hard work.

Artemis says a lot to herself, sitting and holding conversations in her head, and it hardly seems to matter if nobody hears her. In fact, it is better this way.

The second woman is younger, an Englishwoman who came to the village and married a Greek man. She has made her decision and is glad to be settled. Juliet shares with many of the foreign women who stay on in Greece the characteristics of determination, endurance and optimism. She has a daughter, Joanna.

Nobody knows that Juliet keeps a diary but she hopes that her daughter will find it and read it one day, for she believes that a diary should eventually be read by a second person. Such a reading is one method of validating the writer's existence, an existence the reader may have taken for granted, or not even dreamed of. Sometimes, for example, Juliet is a mother, sometimes she is not. Sometimes she is not Kyra Pavlina – Mrs Paul – which is what the old women call her. She has a name of her own, although she rarely hears it. She hopes that one day Joanna will call a daughter after her. She likes the idea. Something to look forward to. Perhaps.

Juliet asks herself why she keeps a diary, examines the reasons for her routine of sitting at the end of a long day, after all her housework and teaching are done, and writing. Often there is not a great deal to write about. Village life is monotonous once its rhythms are established in foreign blood, once the pulse-rates begin to match: the novelty does not take long to wear off. What is the point, after all, of mentioning fast and feast, winter and summer, seed-time and harvest more than once? Juliet supposes she writes because she must. Joanna gives meaning to her life, but shape is needed as well. She is also, she considers, calling across time and space. Listen to me, she is saying, understand me, even if it is too late. Then, too, she needs to mull things over on paper, and in English. Her Greek is more than adequate, but writing and speaking in Greek are never the same, never enough somehow, and Juliet realises that this feeling will not change, will only deepen and become more set with her increasing age.

A diary, Juliet considers, is a document – solidified talk, in a way. She talks, of course, to her friends, in particular in English to her friend Irene. Or she used to. But conversation floats away and is lost. Juliet's diary is always there; she rereads it, often before saying her prayers, and notices how she has managed to struggle through various difficult phases of life, occasionally so successfully that she has forgotten all about them. These reminders help her through the current difficult phase and will help her through the ones to come, for there will always be difficult phases. She is sure of that.

Irene is the third woman, the restless one. She comes and goes, leaving the village and returning to it, which are by no means the same thing. Irene is a teacher and a writer and a reader. She is Australian, although being a wanderer by nature and of necessity she has not lived in Australia for many years. She married a migrant and now has migrated twice because of him, the second time to England.

Irene has no daughters. She loves her three children with the bitter tenderness mothers sometimes reserve for sons, mothers whose boys look at them all too often with the eyes of strangers. And she is racked with pain and guilt over leaving Joachim, her youngest, who is only twelve. She writes to him every single day: the flow of postcards never stops.

Irene posts the pictures: Buckingham Palace, the Guards, Big Ben, the Thames Barrier, the Tower, St Paul's, the series goes on and on. On the back of each card she makes matter-of-fact comments about London and asks Joachim questions about school. This is the pattern that has developed during term-time. A boarding-school situation, say Irene's English friends in their brisk fashion.

But Irene and Joachim never considered boarding-school, and in any case it is Irene who comes home for the holidays. Irene, not a modern woman, feels that it is rather strange for mothers to do this, but everything has been turned on its head and now she can only approximate home. Nothing is the same: Joachim's brothers, Thomas and Michael, also come and go. They, too, are nomads. She cannot blame them for this; she blames herself instead. As usual.

Irene is a wanderer even within cities. She works hard, mainly at writing, but continually ventures out in a regular and disciplined effort to explore London, which has, like Melbourne, been a city of her mind forever. She sits and works in a house in Hampstead, living uneasily as she has always done, she realises one day with a shock, on the edge of other people's lives. But this is a kind family, the one whose flat she occupies; she tries not to get in the way too much. Irene's life is one of patterns, interconnections, synchronicities: she has met this family and is staying in their house because of Amy, her English friend who lives in Melbourne. Amy knows the family, Amy is the link.

A nomad within cities: in her first winter in London Irene lived in Bayswater, and criss-crossed Kensington Gardens for hours at a time in an obsessive ritual disguised as walking a friend's dog. The dog had never been so fit, Irene thinks now with a wry laugh. She herself was fit for nothing.

A r t e m i s They don't realise, the family, that I am still here. They think I am absent all the time but this is not true. They tease me, holding the mirror up to my face, asking me whom I see there. I do not want to recognise myself. Why should I? Once I was beautiful; now look at me: a wrinkled bag of bones, a sack holding my spirit in. One day the sack will fray and wear so much that my spirit will escape and fly away. Then I will be free, at last. Ach, what I have seen – and *not* in this tiny frame they show me.

I have done my best with my children, as a mother must, but sometimes they astonish me. The mirror. All right, it is a joke to them, but to me it is serious, and they ought to *know*. Know about ghosts, know that my soul could be drawn into the mirror and disappear forever. They should hide the mirror. Or cover it. But perhaps they want to get rid of me. I can't blame them. I want to die, but somehow o καλός θάνατος, the good death, is slow in coming. In the meantime, I suppose, when they hold the mirror up to my face I know that something of me, of what I was, is still here.

But at this moment I do not really concern myself with such matters. There are other things more important. The foreign wife, the one my favourite son brought back, has left. At least I think that is what all the φασαρία, the fuss, is about. They are trying to keep it from me, of course, but I am not surprised. I have been waiting a long time for this to happen.

I do not imagine that he, my son, ever loved this foreigner. He loves me, his mother, and his children, as is natural and right. Wives are for work. But this wife, this foreigner, was not. She let us down. She was not built for work. Too slight. Fleet of foot, though, I will give her that. Pity she didn't run away, fast, sooner than this. She tried to live here but I knew she would never succeed. She did not fit, even though she looked a little like us: short, dark of eye and hair. A fairish complexion, though.

Men are men. What did she expect? Men never give their wives their whole attention. Why should they? Wives have their children and their houses and the company of other women. I do not understand why they should want anything else.

My son, the beautiful one, the one who never complained or fought with me, is a good provider. This foreign woman had a roof over her head, food in her stomach. Sons who are παλλικάρια, brave warriors. Three sons, as I have, the first two like trunks of the cypress tree, tall and straight, and the third growing in the same way. My little one, my Ιωακείμ, Joachim. I wanted a girl when he was born. Yes, I did, for I wanted my proud name Artemis to live on. Why not? I was named for the daughter of Zeus, the twin sister of Apollo. Artemis's followers dressed as bears. My father told me all these things: he could read and write, my father.

I even consented to the foreigner giving Joachim two names. Yes, I wanted my name to live but it is not possible to have everything, and he is a good boy, doing his best in the absence of his mother.

She wanted too much, this person. Such women are dangerous. As I have three sons, so I have three daughters-in-law. I can't say that any one of them is perfect. But this one, the most educated, is the stupidest of the three. That's because she's foreign, of course. How we laughed behind our hands at her clumsy efforts. Why did she try to please us? She must have known it would be useless. She did useless things, always pulling bits of paper out of her pocket and scribbling on them. Why I do not know. Neither does God.

Young as she was when I first met her, she wore glasses and her hair was streaked with grey. It was obvious why this was so, but I told her anyway. Too much reading, I said. Too many books. All these things turn the head, addle the brain. She had nothing to say, and that was the pattern later when she came here. I would tell her, scold her, try to teach her, try to make her fit. I had no choice: that is a mother-in-law's work. She would look at me, her flecked, mud-coloured eyes meeting mine briefly, then she would turn away. Once I saw the glitter of tears; perhaps that is why she always turned away. I do not know. I do know that tears are a waste of time, a sign of weakness, and weakness cannot be afforded.

I was opposed to the match from the start. My husband, that soft priest, was far too tolerant. It will be all right, he said. She is a Christian and that is all that matters. Men and their simple minds. Let her learn the language, he added, and it will be all right. He never met her. And then he died. Language. It is not as simple as that; nothing ever is. She never learned to speak it as we speak it, anyway. All these failings. She couldn't even give birth naturally. What a fuss. Hospitals, operations, and she nearly died the last time. They *were* big, though, τα παιδιά, I must say, and the last one the biggest.

Whore. Πουτάνα. It must be so, for she has left, and who would ever leave alone? No woman. This is strange though – for she was never bold. She was shy, not the sort to attract men. But of course it is impossible to tell. It *must* be so, I must be right. No natural woman would ever leave her child. But then she was never natural. She wasted her time wandering and walking. Oh, she did cook and clean and knit but she liked doing other things better. Yes, there must be a man, although this I can never understand. The embrace of a child, your own child, is pure and lasts longer. Every woman knows that.

This one, I must say, eventually came to love the place. More than I did. She loved those harsh mountains as I never could; she gathered wildflowers and brought me posies, knowing that I liked them. But still she left.

I do not know what happened exactly, what went wrong. It took a long time, as I have said. The women saw her crying, sobbing, gasping, and not just once, in the κτήματα, there in the fields for all to see. The disgrace of it. As a family, we were ruined.

Better she were dead. Death is as natural and as right as birth. It is easier to bear than disgrace. She waited, I know she did, until I started to fail, for she had no spirit. She would never have dared to leave had I my old strength. Nor would she dare to come back. Her return is certain, because of the child. She is, when all is said and done, a mother.

J u l i e t   Tonight there is an awful lot to write about. Joanna must have heard, although we didn't mention the matter at dinner. Her father is deeply shocked and doesn't want to discuss what has happened. He can't believe it: that's obvious from the look of bewilderment on his face. I can hardly believe it myself, although the signs were there. But often signs flutter, make a great show, and then come to nothing. I could kick myself now, when I think of them.

Tomorrow I will have to tell Joanna properly that her friend Joachim's mother has left. She's gone to England and nobody knows when or if she'll be back. She's obviously having some sort of breakdown. I'm hurt, yes I am, that she didn't tell me, didn't take me into her confidence.

Irene's my friend. How could she do this? We've known each other so long, have so much in common, even though I'm English and she's Australian. Greeks think that that means we're exactly the same, that we're interchangeable or something, but of course that's wrong.

The unifying thing is that we're the foreign wives of Greek men, the mothers of Greek children – half-Greek, to be accurate, although it's always seemed to me that the Greek half is more than a half, is dominant. What are the words to describe this domination? Does the Greek part smother, suffocate, crush, repress or drown the other half? I don't know; all I know is that the combination of heredity and environment is very nearly invincible. Yet every so often, as I look at Joanna and Joachim, good friends and close in age, I see something non-Greek in them: a fleeting expression, an unexpected reaction of some sort. It's difficult to explain; many things, let's face it, are difficult to explain.

When I was about seventeen, I thought it was only a matter of time before most important things would be clear, would become comprehensible. When I finished school, when I got married, when we built the house, when we had a baby . . . I moved past expecting happiness though, and now, a good thirty years since I was seventeen, I have given up on clarity as well. We all – but particularly displaced women, it seems to me – just muddle on. I'm quite content to muddle on, at least I think I am. Certainly I know I could never do what Irene's done. We're the same age, she and I; it's too late to start again. Surely she knows there are no encores in life? I love her dearly, but she's mad if she hasn't learned this lesson. She'll learn it the hard way now, I bet.

I never thought she'd do it, never thought she'd leave, although I watched and watched her over the years and saw her spirit dwindling, saw her body becoming thinner and thinner, her face paler, lined and anxious, with its eyes growing ever larger. I watched and worried. We talked, we were always talking, but clearly our talks, our friendship, were not enough.

She wanted a different life, that was obvious, and had had one once upon a time in Australia. I consider that a major problem, actually, the fact that she didn't start her married life in the village. It might've been better if she had. If. If . . . Who knows? But the honeymoon stage and the lingering memory of it can get you through all sorts of difficult times. Irene was long past that stage when she arrived here. She already had two children, and, it seems to me now, had already been badly hurt. Those wounds never quite healed, would gape and bleed again. She needed to grow another skin, actually, but she didn't seem able to. She's not one to take life easily. Never was, that seems obvious.

Greece enchanted her, though. Well, it enchants us all. What a place: it gets to you and it is hard to explain why. I've tried for twenty years to explain it, and tonight I'm too tired and upset to start all over again. I never seem to get any further, never seem to find an answer. Greece enchanted her, and her husband was almost deliriously happy to be back and so she tried. She really did try, and for a long time. I had never seen him so happy, she said once. Sadly.

Why did she leave? There's never one answer to a question like that. The death of her mother in Melbourne? Perhaps. She got there in time, having feared she wouldn't, but was a deeply changed person when she returned. I thought so, anyway.

Of course she wasn't fortunate in having the mother-in-law she did. The contrast with her own mother was hard to cope with. Old Artemis was aptly named: a huntress who knew her mark, who didn't need to sniff the air twice to scent a victim.

All that's changed now; the old harridan's on another planet. Or is she? Sometimes I wonder. There's a snapping in her eyes that I notice on my occasional visits. She's always been a wily one. She wore Irene down, I think, and then out. She wasn't kind, but then kindness is a rare commodity here.

Suddenly I feel very tired and can hardly push the pen along. Don't let me get sick again, God. People don't realise that living in Greece can seriously endanger your health. All those summer Adonises should be forced to wear an appropriate label around their necks: FOREIGN GIRLS, BEWARE. Greece and Greekness are far worse for your heart than smoking, and your soul is at risk too. To be fair to this place though, it isn't just Greece that threatens: any form of exile is dangerous. Displaced people die by inches. Yes, inches. I refuse to say centimetres, because I'm English and I want to resist Europe – in a small way at least.

A r t e m i s   She's back. I can tell. There is something in the air; the atmosphere, the feeling, has changed. There is a buzz of conversation in the room and it is not the usual one. Of course I knew she would return, for that is the way mothers are and have to be. But had I my old strength, I would never allow her back. What is my son thinking of? But wait: for once you're wrong, old woman. He's thinking of Joachim, naturally.

Joachim, *my* Joachim, came today; I think he probably comes every day but I do not always realise he is here. Sometimes there are other people about, and only the good God knows who they are for I certainly do not most of the time. But occasionally there is a kind of click or flash, something I don't understand, and then I see and I know again.

He teases me, Joachim, about my oil, that precious

thing which I have had to guard and eke out all my life. I snap at him, but it is just a game we play. I think, hope, he knows that, for I would not hurt him. It is difficult for me to be gentle; it always has been difficult because life is not soft, not easy. Because of that we cannot always be as we would wish. I would like my Joachim to know how much I love him but the expression of love does not come easily to me.

Before, there was not time for such things, and now, when I should be able to let go a little, when my greatest problem is how to fill time, that yawning, endless space, I do not know how to say what I feel, and cannot hold the thread of thought long enough in any case. What I feel is a surge of life when Joachim is in the room. This is the beauty, the value of children. Perhaps he knows I come alive when he is here. I hope so.

I also hope that she, his mother, knows what I think of her. She probably does, as I never did hide my opinion of her. Right from the start my feeling was that she could never be trusted. Strangers never can be, can never be relied upon to do the right thing. Foreigners are always fated. Difference does not do. Foreigners do not know what we know: even that postman who works here, the one from ten kilometres away, had no idea at first that I am a priest's widow, a παπαδιά, and used to bellow at the door for Kyría Artemis – Mrs Artemis. Ignoramus. Παπαδιά is my proper title.

The foreign wife, the nífi, would do the same thing.

15

Πάλι, ignoramus. Proud she was, and determined to be called by her own name. Proud, I said, but in the wrong way – proud of herself. A woman should be proud to be called by her husband's name; a woman should be proud of her family. She should have looked to her house, this one. Τρέχει η γηναίκα και δεν φτάνει. A woman's work is never done. Everybody knows that: that is the way things are.

It is still not clear to me why she left. She grieved dreadfully for her mother, I know that. She liked to keep things hidden from me, always liked to keep herself to herself, but she could not hide the fact that she was in deep distress when her mother died. This is natural and right: I remember my grief for my own mother, so suddenly taken from me.

The grief of the foreigner was overdone. Her mother had a good death in hospital, in comfort, with medicine and nurses always at hand. She did not have to endure this awful, drawn-out business I am going through, with all these threads fraying. But she was much younger than I, the foreigner's mother. Perhaps she was not ready; perhaps she was frightened. At my age I am only frightened of living, of life dragging on too long. Try as I might, there is nothing I can do to speed things. Think what this fortunate woman, now at peace and at rest, was spared. It is said she was not Orthodox though, and this is something which it is impossible for me to understand. Perhaps she is not at peace after all, or does not know the peace I am bound to know when my time comes.

Even though she was foreign I liked her. She was a pretty woman, a kind woman, a lady. She was respectable and she did her best to talk to me in her poor, ugly Greek with its thick and heavy accent. But although I liked her I always wondered about her, for there was a light in her eye which I did not fully understand. It was part of her foreignness: she had seen other places, known other ways. It is likely that she encouraged her daughter in that particular wilfulness which made the latter leave, and just as surely made her return.

I am concentrating and listening, holding fast to my thoughts, but I have not heard a whisper about a man. Yet it is still the most likely explanation for her leaving. Passion: a foolish word to dwell on at my age. Of course I've heard about it, in songs and scandal, but have never wanted any part of it, for passion and death go together. Here in these mountain villages, παλιά, a long time ago, the occasional couple would elope. Search parties – and there were always search parties, for were not land and honour involved? – would drag the wells before they did anything else. More than one deluded couple wanted to be together in death.

Yes, passion and death go together, so passion is to be avoided, as we have no hope of avoiding death. It, passion, also sounds exhausting, and is life not exhausting enough? Passion is for the foolish, as is discontent.

I sit here and wonder whether Joachim's mother will stay. I do not know. There is nothing for me to do but wait and see.

J u l i e t   I've seen Irene and will see her again; I'll probably see her every day. But it won't be easy, she isn't saying much. Most of the time she merely looks at me with drained eyes. She's not happy. Of course not, how could she be? Did she expect to be? It's impossible to build happiness on others' pain, and equally impossible to build it on your own. I don't know what the answer is, unless it's to cross happiness off the list. Either that, or to find happiness in the situation that exists. Sometimes you have to dig deeply for that, sometimes not. Joanna's my happiness; I could never leave her, and she's never thought of the possibility, not even now. Perhaps that's the difference between having daughters and having sons. I'm not sure. Then there's Pavlos. He's maddening. Well, they all are. But he loves me in his fashion, I know he does.

Men, poor things, do not understand women's needs. Pavlos has very little understanding of Joanna, and his obtuseness will get worse as she grows. He loves her blindly. And hurts her terribly. Pavlos is one of those men who bond with their mothers and with their children. Wives? Well, every man has to have a wife. That's the done thing. If men do not marry, the world will think they are not men. Lovers? This also seems to be the done thing: once again men need to prove they're men, I suppose. Who cares? I don't. Pavlos always comes back to me. In fact, he never goes away. What does it matter if he stays out late now and then, as long as I don't know the details? I have my security and never want to give it up. I've worked too hard for it. He'll never leave me. I do know *that*.

Men cling on to power always, but of course women are far more powerful than men and part of that power is being prepared to let it go. A paradox. Childbirth is all about this paradox, surely? Men gibber with fear at the thought of childbirth, or else they toss off thoughts of the whole business very lightly. Natural, isn't it? they say, so what's all the fuss about? It's about life and power, that's what. A pregnant woman has great power but is taken over by a power greater than she is, and during the process of childbirth is both in control and out of it. She has to rely on other people, as some of us have to at the time of our death. If things go very wrong, as they did when Joachim was born, she has to give her very life into the hands of others.

That loss of freedom. The irony of it. Once you're a mother you can never be free again. The power lies in the fact that you have a soul and spirit in your keeping, but you mustn't ever abuse that power. Your reward is in watching the child grow. A woman hopes for bearable pain, followed by a healthy child. The traditional setting for pain, power and death for men is war, and that setting is all cluttered up with ghastly concepts like patriotism. No country is worth my sons' lives, Irene said once, and she's right.

It's difficult having her back. She's told me that she won't stay but that she wants to spend the summer with Joachim. She's never been out of touch with him: he shows Joanna most of the postcards. When can we go to London? she says. When indeed?

It's difficult having Irene back because in my heart I feel she's let the side down. We, the foreign wives, consider, as a general thing, that we're all in this together and we all ought to pull together. She's breached our solidarity in a way. It's true that we fantasise about doing what she did. We'll stage a mass walk-out, we tell each other, usually when we're slightly in our cups, and *that'll* show them. Oh yes, we talk about it, but we haven't done it. She has. I hate to think of the guilt and loneliness she must be experiencing now. She did tell me that when she arrived at Heathrow all those months ago, more dead than alive, she saw three English mothers with three half-Greek babies in the airport bus and burst into tears at the thought of what could happen to all six of them. Weeping in public, that wasn't her style at all.

But I know she cried inside, frequently, for we all do. Some of us cannot do otherwise, and Joachim's mother was one of them. I don't think her husband ever understood that it's the patient ones who wear out. I do my share of crying inside, but in general I've given up playing the part of the restrained middle-class lady. I've forgotten my lines, have assumed a new role: I shriek like a Billingsgate fish-wife, I throw tantrums. It's the only thing to do. I tried to get Irene to do the same. Lose your temper, I used to tell her. Throw wobblies, big ones. Roar and rage. But she wasn't made that way. She's quiet, shy, ladylike and obedient, all these things. Not everybody saw the intensity that's also there. And now look what's happened.

She hasn't breathed a word about why she left. I still think her mother's death was the main factor, it made her think about life being short. The wingéd chariot and all that. So she acted. After all, when it's time, it's time.

Whatever the final straw was, the camel's back was very ready to break and did. People said she'd met someone else. I doubt it, for she's never mentioned anybody to me, and we've known each other for ages, have helped each other through many a bad patch.

I'm still trying to help her but I'm failing. Perhaps nobody can help her. Of course we're very different, she and I. She said that once. She sounded wistful and I thought she envied me rather. She's chosen the jungle, I the prison. Still, I do what I like; nobody bosses *me* about.

I must add, though, that one part of me, the part that thinks she's let the side down, wonders what all the fuss is about. Men are men and not inclined to be faithful. It's a difficult life here and Greek ethics are different, but so what? It could be worse. You have to compromise in this world and look out for number one. Greeks are good at that. I'm not bad at it myself. Idealism, innocence, naïveté, all of which are part of Irene's makeup, have to be grown out of. You mustn't expect too much. It can only lead to disappointment. If people hurt you, punish them, not yourself. Irene is punishing herself, it seems to me.

I'm tired, as usual, and must stop writing. But sometimes fatigue makes thought clearer, focuses images more sharply, and it has just occurred to me that Irene and Greece are like ouzo and ice, while I'm like ouzo with water. Ouzo and water merge instantaneously, but ice resists ouzo, retaining its shape for quite some time before breaking down into flaky crystals.

Yes, that's it: resistance. Resistance and the breaking down.

I r e n e We have had the summer together, Joachim and I. The end of August is not just the end of a month – it is the start of a new season. There is a distinct change of mood: life becomes serious again. Now it is September. I am sitting at my desk and thinking about Joachim. Sometimes I wonder whether I think about anything or anybody else. But I cannot afford, very often, to think about the other inhabitant of my heart, for he does not want to dwell there. And so I think about Joachim. Constantly.

I have never spent September in England before, and most of me still lingers with Joachim in the village – in that other, very familiar, Greek autumn.

In November Joachim will have his thirteenth birthday. Already he is stretching from child to man, becoming long and spindly; the shape of his face is changing, his bones becoming more prominent as the last layers of baby fat melt away. Now he has bands on his teeth and he wiggles the plate that annoys him so much. He wants a particular style of haircut, shaved at the back, long locks at the front, but Vasili, his father, says no. On hearing the firm *oxi*, Joachim's lids drop like shutters over rebellious grey eyes.

I recite these details in a ritual naming of parts. I do not want to be away from Joachim. I do not cope with separations well, with this one least of all. But this one, for all sorts of complicated reasons, was inevitable. And so we say our goodbyes, lightly, casually, as best we can. We share, when all is said and done, that heritage of the stiff upper lip. We say, 'See you soon,' and do our best to smile. For years I have heard in every hallo the echo of goodbye; now I try mightily to reverse that echo, but do not dare to ask whether he can hear it.

So it will soon be thirteen years since Joachim was born in Athens. It will soon be fifty years since I was born in Melbourne, and nearly fifteen years have passed since I came to live in the village, which is the only place he has ever called home. It is very hard to believe in a time when one did not exist. Joachim always did exist, I am convinced of that, because I am sure he tried to arrive a few years earlier. I never stopped wanting him, and he finally arrived, my Greek child. Vasili was surprised. I was surprised only by geography: the other boys were born in Melbourne.

The experts seem to agree that memories begin to be stored at about the age of three. That is when I began my particular filing system. It has been said that the purpose of life is to remember, and this thought comforts me, as I seem to spend a great deal of time remembering. I seem unable to cultivate the art of forgetting: in that respect I am a slow learner.

So I must have been three and it must have been spring in Melbourne on the day I rode my tricycle at what I was sure was breakneck speed down Paxton Street, East Malvern. My grandmother and her brother were walking up the street, and the plane trees were already forming a canopy overhead. A pattern has evolved, as patterns do in the course of a lifetime: that street is only a short distance from the place where my mother died recently and a long time ago now. Death and falling in love both have the effect of distorting time, as Joachim will discover for himself.

The final separation. At the time of my mother's death I did not notice the plane trees. The jacarandas and the flowering gums claimed my small spare attention, for I had not spent a summer in Melbourne for many years and I had been a different person way back then.

Joachim's birthday. Of course I'll give him more than one present, as I always do, but I want to give him one that will last, for his whole life has been a present to me. If I persist, this present, the collection of letters, should be ready by November. Some I am writing to him now; some I wrote to his grandparents from Greece while I waited for him; some were written to me by Amy, whom Joachim met more than once in Melbourne.

He last met her on his name-day, one September the ninth, and Amy gave him, as we left, an envelope to open in the tram. Inside the envelope was a twenty-dollar note.

'What a relief,' he said, and laughed. 'Now I don't have to worry about Thomas's twenty-first birthday next week. I can give him this.' I shouldn't have been surprised but I was, and my heart, a mother's heart, gave a great lurch.

'Are you sure?' I asked.

'Of course,' he grinned, and then I had to stare fixedly out of the tram window lest my tears disgrace him.

That tug of love for a child. There is nothing to be done about it. On that same visit to Melbourne I met an old *yiayia* in a bus shelter. The bravery of her. She had emigrated at the age of sixty-five from a village near Thessaloniki in order to be near her children, who lived somewhere near the Chadstone Shopping Centre. The day I met her she was on her way to visit her husband in hospital. She knew the colour of the bus and the name of its destination, and little else. Of course she asked me pressing questions about my life story, so I sketched it briefly: how I'd met Joachim's father when I was quite young and how I had eventually gone to live in a Peloponnesian village. She gave me a sad smile. 'The things we do for love, παιδάκι μου, my little child,' she sighed.

And now? And now I think, The things we do in spite of love, even though it is the only enchantment we know. Love, like birth and death, is inevitable and involuntary. We tend, older people, often to forget this, but are occasionally reminded, as I was a while ago when I fell very unexpectedly but quite desperately in love with a man who did not fall in love with me. I must point out to Joachim that unrequited love is much less common between parents and children:

26

mothers, at least, are usually poleaxed. This is a necessary occurrence, otherwise we poor things would
never stay the course, could never cope with that life
sentence of worry and yearning.

I long, often, to talk to Joachim about these things,
but dare not, cannot. I want to tell him of Sylvia Plath's
poem about a newborn baby – 'Love set you going like
a fat gold watch' – but I have a vision of him looking at
me quizzically, ironically, and then saying tolerantly,
'Ye-es, Mum,' grinning at the mere idea of poetry, and
poetry in English at that.

Of course the letters will be too much; I know I
tend to overdo things. That is the way I am. Perhaps
he'll read them at some later stage. Perhaps I am writing them for myself? It has been said that in order to
see where you're going, you have to look back and see
where you've been. I have not the remotest idea where
I'm going: I dream of being lost, of losing my passport,
of going blind. I wake up panicking and muttering
lines of Shakespeare: 'The bright day is done and we
are for the dark.' So I'm looking back, preparing these
letters, in the hope that the recollection of bright days,
and there were many, will light my way forward just a
little further. The journey *is* ever onward, after all.

But now I want to be back with Joachim in the village, in the Greek autumn. I want to be back with
Juliet, too. She's my friend. I miss her but I do not
understand her, although I envy her greatly. She is

where she wants to be, that seems certain, but she puts up with a great deal, in my opinion. *That* makes me feel guilty. Why couldn't I put up with everything? Juliet is fortunate that she can do so.

Doesn't she want to be free, though? How can she stand being in the power of Pavlos, who is never home, yet controls everything and everybody, upsets Joanna regularly, and for whom Juliet works like a dog? You're forgetting something, I tell myself. Juliet is loved and feels herself to be. A woman, our type of woman, can live forever and put up with anything if she has that certainty. And a man can get away with murder – well, almost – if he can convince our type of woman that she is loved. It's as simple as that.

How far is will involved? Perhaps it doesn't come into it at all. I do not know. What I do know is that I want to be back there. With Juliet. With Joachim. Now.

Wandering Irene finds it impossible to travel light, even when merely setting out for Hampstead Heath. She takes pen and pencil, notebook, at least one slim packet of old letters written to her parents to pore over, and her current reading matter all stuffed into a black cloth bag, Vikram Seth's *A Suitable Boy* doing damage to her shoulders. She tramps the Heath or wanders the streets of Belsize Park, talking aloud to herself, but quietly, for she does not want to be taken for a bag lady. She is, when all is said and done, a suit-case lady.

She remembers that winter past in Bayswater when all she did was walk and walk: the unfamiliar trees skeined in mist, the layers of fog with figures merging into and emerging from whiteness, the ghostliness of it all. She remembers the strange appropriateness of that time, that place, for her life was not at all in focus and all her mind was clouded with doubt. Everywhere she went she looked – was always searching for – something, anything, to plug the gap of loss. But whenever she saw little boys feeding ducks or sailing boats on the ruffled surface of the iron-grey pond, she knew that the search would have no end, that nothing would heal her of her grievous wound, for rescue and peace were not to be found in Kensington Gardens or anywhere else.

There are always solitaries on the Heath, but Irene will not notice them. There is no possibility of her becoming chatty with a total stranger up here where the kites are dipping and soaring. Total strangers never approach her, anyway. Though she is chirpily, relent-lessly bright when surrounded by invited company, her natural reaction to people is one of flight and retreat. She wants, quite simply, to disappear. Irene is a shy person.

She sits and looks at the mighty heart of London, puzzling over the skyline, working out the landmarks. She sits, reads, makes notes and thinks, most often about the past. She writes letters. She has always conducted an enormous correspondence and finds it difficult to refrain from letter writing. Some of her correspondents have now died, doubtless in self-defence, she thinks a trifle ruefully. But usually Irene does not think much about her writing: it is merely something she does, and it has not occurred to her to consider letters as revenge, letters as an invasion of privacy, letters as a demand. Look at me, do not forget me, I won't *let* you forget me. It has crossed her mind that letters are a form of compensation, have some connection with her sense of self: for Irene, so long an invisible woman, they have been a means of becoming and remaining visible. She must remain visible to Joachim, or die. When she is not writing new ones, Irene goes through her old letters a few at a time. Her parents accumulated boxes of them, each bearing beautiful stamps — heraldic in colour and variety and intensity. In the winter of 1975/6, the time of Irene's first visit to Greece, the stamps depicted traditional costumes: women in graceful skirts, aprons and scarves; men wearing the fustanella or Cretan breeches. Irene handles the envelopes carefully, for the stamps might be valuable.

She has always had a weakness for elegant stationery, but it was a struggle to find any sort of paper in the village. She holds that very first letter she wrote from Greece and remembers that the paper it was written on had been pulled out of an exercise book. The edge of each page is badly tattered and torn. Her handwriting has changed since then: these days it's smaller and more erratic, much like Irene herself.

In this first letter Irene expressed amazement at being unable to find any aerogrammes. Eventually she was able to buy some old ones. She knew they were old because on each blue cover the king's head had been scratched out: it had been somebody's job to scribble blue biro over the relevant spot. Irene still feels sorry for ex-King Constantine, another displaced person now living, she has heard, in Hampstead Garden Suburb.

Among the letters is a picture that Irene's middle son, Michael, drew of the village when he was seven, after the whole family had gone to live there. This picture, Irene thinks, shows everything: the powerful sun, the token two clouds, the toothy mountains edged with olive trees, the cross-roads. And two buildings – Yiayia's, her mother-in-law's, house, and her own. A child's world, Irene knows now, not big enough for an adult who had lived in and loved another.

Today is today and Irene is sitting, old letters held firmly against the wind, gazing out over the great city, while part of her travels back to other times, to other places.

I r e n e   It is hard to believe now that I did not leave Australia until I was thirty. It is embarrassing to remember what a sheltered, heedless girl I was then. Yes, girl – in spite of work, marriage, domesticity, two children and the constant, uneasy shift, even in Melbourne, between a Greek world and an Australian one. The Greek world was a type of layer, I thought, not the real thing. Later I thought of it as a graft – one that did not take. Even later still I think that the graft has taken all too well. My favourite line of Greek poetry was written by George Seferis: it leapt out at me once from a book I found, strangely, on a Melburnian bookshelf. <<Όπου και να ταξιδέψω, η Ελλάδα με πληγώνει>> 'Wherever I travel, Greece wounds me.' Sometimes I think there is nothing more to add to that, nothing more to be said, but still I persist in this sorting-out, problem-solving business.

Of course I go back to Greece, in spite of the wounds, for I cannot live without Joachim for very long. But it is hard when I go back. All those eyes which flick away at my approach. People think the worst and give me no credit for my efforts, for all the years I stayed and struggled. Leaving and returning are very different things.

I do not know what Joachim thinks, but the villagers think I left because of a man. They think I've a lover. Would it were true. I did not leave because of a man: there was no one waiting to meet me in London. We are born, we die, we migrate, and sometimes we love, alone. The person I love does not love me, and there's an end to the matter. There is nothing more to say, except that I loved him against reason and against hope, and still do; he is in my heart and mind but not in my life.

It seems to me we leave our known worlds not for one reason but for very many, which, usually over a long period, pile up and begin to exert pressure. When it's time, it's time. Some day Joachim will understand these things. I am not sure what to say to him now.

Time. The Christmas of 1975: Thomas and Michael were tiny. Thomas, now impossibly grand and a man of twenty-two with a car, a girlfriend and a suit, not necessarily in that order of importance, was then aged three and three months and was a *trial*. Not to mention a nuisance and a demanding pest. Lovable, too, of course, especially when he was asleep, a happy state of affairs which did not occur too often. Sleep appeared to be against his religion.

Michael, now a cadet in the Greek army, was then only thirteen months, but much more placid than Thomas. Joachim and Michael are very much alike: quiet, busy, interested, with wide smiles and good senses of humour. They are also prone to fits of filthy temper and the sulks. Like their mother, I'm ashamed to say.

That very first letter.

December 1975
I am enjoying it all, in spite of worrying about
Thomas, who is sleeping a lot, but in snatches,
a sure sign of worry, and am missing my
creature comforts (like a bath!) very much.

Then, there was only a cold-water tap in the yard. Much later, the boys' aunt Penelope used to tell the story of an old man who was cross with his daughter-in-law because she had insisted on installing a hot-water service in the house where three generations lived together.

'I don't actually mind,' he said, 'but it's October, late October, isn't it? Whoever heard of having a bath during the winter?'

Here people tell me tales of Scottish farmers greasing themselves all over with mutton-fat and then being sewn into their clothes for the duration of the cold weather.

Thomas has always been attached to place and is now attached to two, a real dilemma. The older boys will always have this problem. When in Australia they will miss Greece, and vice versa. But Joachim has only

34

ever had one home. The other places are for holidays. He has not been uprooted the way they were. I am glad of that.

It's a great experience and helps one to realise what a free, untrammelled life some people lead. As Vasili says, people here haven't any hooks in them, whereas we have hundreds!

I didn't know then what I know now. Now I am older and wiser and much, much sadder. What a simplistic view of things Vasili and I had then.

But then I believed in a mysterious expansion of my world, which had changed its shape and admitted all sorts of differences. I noted the physical details: the little white houses strung along the street, the dark caverns of shops, the congregations of men whose eyes would follow me stonily as I walked past. They wondered who the jeans-clad foreigner was, but had me placed within three minutes, I learned later. Donkeys puffed under the weight of branches and sacks of olives; goats teetered and tottered, coping as best they might with swollen udders. In Yiayia's kitchen I admired the bamboo-lined roof and charcoal-blackened beams, and laughed off, later, the showers of dust and hail which fell through the gaps and spaces.

My education broadened there in the village, I

must admit. And I am glad of it. The olive press was just across the road. I observed it at work and began to have a glimmer of understanding about the peasants' attachment to their olive trees. They call them roots, ρίζες, more often than trees, and I thought that very revealing. Unshaven, bleary-eyed young men worked constantly, driving tractors, collecting full bags, heaving them about inside the press.

The lights there burned for much of the night. I fell asleep to the pulsing of the machinery; the smell of new oil hung in the air. In the mornings I ate that same new oil on toast, and am still addicted to it, to that catch and burning at the back of the throat. I rode Yiayia's donkey and didn't fall off, but I rode astride, which was, and remains, not the done thing: an old widow made it quite clear that she did not approve of my wearing trousers.

That first time was only a holiday, so the heating of water and the washing by hand were bearable, for I would soon be back in appliance-eased suburbia. But I froze in the biting winds and severe frosts, and deeply resented the power cuts that reduced my reading time. Until they experience it, nobody ever believes how cold and wet the Peloponnese can be, and how the weather can still affect, very easily, the most basic of services.

Thomas was wiser than I and suffered from immediate culture shock. He became aggressive, demanding, tearful, homesick, wakeful, and went off his food. He also got into mischief.

January 1976

A neighbouring child took Thomas down to a rabbit hutch belonging to old Maria, who lives next door. The child opened the door of the hutch and gave Thomas a bucket of water, whereupon he 'christened' the rabbits. We discovered this when we met Maria on her way to light a fire in order to warm the poor creatures. Fortunately she blames the other child, who is six.

It is a warm, sunny day. Michael is asleep. Thomas is amusing himself on the terrace and the other grown-ups, Yiayia included, are out harvesting olives. I hope it is the last day of the olive harvest, as I find this a difficult place in which to cope on my own. This morning Thomas disappeared completely and it took me half an hour to find him. Although I can communicate quite well, I feel a bit helpless when things go wrong. And while I'm watching Michael on these awful stairs I never know what Thomas is up to. One day he broke three newly laid eggs and another day he tried to feed the donkey with some eggs and a five-drachma piece.

Both boys have developed a passion for the donkey. Thomas can look after himself quite adequately, or has so far, but Michael tries to poke the donkey in the nostrils and to rub noses with it. The poor beast is very patient, but I wouldn't like to try him too far.

I can't remember now whether Joachim was ever like this. Probably not, as goats and donkeys were so much part of his world that he took them for granted. He was and is very interested in birds and animals, though, and liked seeing the elephants being taken for a walk at Regent's Park zoo. But the Melbourne zoo is better, he said, and so is the Healesville Sanctuary, much better.

It was at the end of a day at the Melbourne zoo that I realised, once again, my children are simply not Australian. Our friend Margaret had taken us to the zoo, as she always does, and the day had been a good one. We were walking back along a quiet path when Margaret said suddenly, 'Oh look, there's a sight you don't often see now, more's the pity. See that speckled thrush?' We looked and there he was, a delicate but busy creature, sorting through the leaves to see what he could find.

'Pretty, aren't they?' Margaret commented.

'They're *so* delicious, too,' Joachim added fervently.

Margaret threw me a look. I tried to gaze into the

middle distance. Joachim's antennae are finely tuned: he *knew*, a second later, what he had said, and looked rueful. Two seconds later, I laughed and learned all over again that I loved him to bits.

We had a brief time together, Joachim and I, on our return to Greece, and then I left again. Leaving him is like an amputation, a very messy one; the stump keeps on bleeding and the phantom pain is no phantom. I keep applying bandages and then ripping them off again.

Suddenly I cannot stay here any longer, here where children and their fathers are flying kites. I fold my letters, draw a line in my notebook, and set off down Parliament Hill.

A r t e m i s   She has gone again, Joachim's mother. Gone to England, they say. I do not know where England is or how one gets there. Perhaps it is attached to Greece, perhaps not. Full of foreigners it is, I know that much. But they did help us, the English, during the war, I must say that. I remember seeing them. There were others who helped us, too: the Australians and New Zealanders. I went εξωτερικό, over the seas to Australia, once. What a time! I went to visit my son and his foreign wife. I did not want to go, but I went. For my child's sake. That is what he wanted. I certainly did not want to stay. I wanted my home, my πατρίδα. The language in Australia was not mine: I could not understand the patterns of the language, the place, the people.

It is always so, surely? Goodbyes mean grief, and surely there is enough grief in life without bringing it on yourself? Why leave a country? Why leave a child? Children leave you soon enough. My foreign daughter-in-law left her natural place, her country, and now she has left her child. We were her family here, but this was not enough. I knew it would not, could not, be. She yearned for other places, other people.

A heretic, of course she was, with no thought of the sacred example of the Holy Family. She never converted, and I always found myself smiling, but bitterly, during the part of the liturgy in which the priest bids heretics begone. She was already there, inside the church, watching Joachim, a beautiful altar boy, and thinking God knows what heathen thoughts. She will be punished sooner or later, as is only natural and right. Παλιά, in the old days, husbands used to punish their wives by putting them down the family well for a few hours. It is a great pity my son is too soft to try it. Soft, like his father. They were obedient, the wives, after that. It is hard to decide on the worst part of that punishment: the fear, the darkness, the cold or the solitude.

And now this unnatural woman has chosen solitude. Well, perhaps, that is still unknown. But she has chosen separation from her child, when she should have sacrificed everything for his sake. Instead she seems to be weaving her own selfish pattern, coming and going, just when my Joachim needs her most, set as he is on the road to manhood. But fate weaves its lessons into the cloth: she will see this, even if she never learns.

I see things clearly now, at my great age: when the flashes come, that is, and when I feel I am in control. Hearing helps, and used to be more important, but the things I hear now often seem muddled and unclear. I don't think the foreigner ever saw anything clearly. How could she hope to, in a place not hers? She didn't know anything when she came here, and she still doesn't know anything.

People said, How wonderful, an educated daughter-in-law. That was all they knew. A useless millstone. She never learned to make cheese, had no idea how to milk a goat, and I had to teach her how to plant garlic. Which end goes in the ground? she asked. Ντροπή της! The shame of it. It has to be said that the other two *nífes* are not much better, taking my sons away from me. Oh, they came back, as sons do come back to their mothers. So they should; this is the way it must be. But it is not the same. We think, we old *yiayiáthes*, that we continue to tread the path worn by our grandmothers and mothers before us. Ναι και όχι. Yes and no. Things change.

Things change over a lifetime, I've learned that.

But why bring change about when it is bound to happen? Birth, death, accident, war. Why *choose* change? Why did she come here? She could have found someone else, or her parents could have forbidden the whole match and arranged another. Nor do I understand why my son wanted to do things differently. The result is a load of grief and three half-foreign children. Still, it must be said that they are good boys. Δόξα το θεό. Glory to God. So far.

They – the women, the family, I don't know who – say that she, the foreigner, writes to my Joachim nearly every day. What good is that? She is not here.

J u l i e t Irene did say she wouldn't stay. She has an unbearable restlessness about her – all part of her unhappiness, I suppose. There's a lot to be said for living a prescribed life, for not having any choice. At least you save energy that way. I'm sure this is one reason for the long lives of the old village women, who plough their age-old furrows in accepting tranquillity, in certain hope of a better life beyond the grave. There's a particular stillness about them which we, the foreign wives, all envy.

My religion consoles me. I can't do without it, and so I talk to God for long periods every day. Sometimes I ask questions which don't seem to be answered, although they will be one day, I'm sure of that. But often it's a case of taking a deep breath and saying, Get me through this, God, please! And invariably I do get through it, whatever the trial is.

Faith is something about which my friend appears to be very unsure. I don't mean to say that she hasn't any, but she's a doubter, a questioner. She kicks a lot. 'Wobbly' is her word for it. It seems to me that she had to rebel against her nonconformist grandmothers, their rigidity. Her marriage could have been part of all that, but that's just my theory. My other theory is that this complicated nonconformist background left her unable to compromise. It also left her completely unable to cope with peasant deviousness, with the practical ruthlessness that is so much part of life here. She's not really grown up, Irene. For a long time, I think, she pretended these things didn't exist. But you can't do that. You've got to adapt, you can't pretend.

She blamed herself for a very long time and is probably still doing so, only for different reasons. She thought she wasn't working hard enough, wasn't making enough effort to fit in. She blamed herself, as we all do, for being discontented. She compared herself with other foreign wives who were putting up with much more, and felt guilty. Perhaps it's fair to say that she was not as tolerant, as patient, as tactful as she might have been, but towards the end she was sure she was dying. 'I'm suffocating,' she'd say, or, 'I'm drowning. They're crushing my spirit, I don't know who I am any more.' She wasn't a fighter. This summer she confessed that on average she used to throw a tantrum a year. 'And then,' she said with a slight grin, 'I'd have to go to bed to recover.' I didn't know this, even though we talked about all sorts of things.

Of course she thought too much, and read too much. You can upset yourself this way; she certainly did. Every so often, though, I have to admit, her quotations were relevant. Late one autumn afternoon we were out walking along a mountain track in that rose light we both love so well, and she quoted Paul Scott to me. We'd all been mad about Paul Scott's novels, the *Raj Quartet* and all that, especially the bit about the migrant tapping forever at the window of his past. But on that particular day she quoted from *Staying On*.

'Lucy Smalley, if I remember rightly, says to Tusker, "You have always deprived me of the fullness of my life in order to support and sustain the smallness of your own."'

Something like that, at any rate. That struck me, I admit, and I gave a strangled laugh and said, 'There's a lot of *that* about, isn't there?'

So she's chosen a larger life, although I can't think it's a happier one, or even a fuller one. It must be quite empty without Joachim. No news of a man. If she did leave because of a man he can't be part of her life now, at least not in any significant way. She would have told me. Men aren't worth the effort, anyhow, and are all alike in their refusal to face their own wounds. But then attachment is a problem for her: she is that sort, the loving sort. Why people here didn't understand this, I don't know. She would have done anything for her husband for a very long time. And how she copes with her separation from Joachim is beyond me. The flow of postcards has started again: she's doing her best. But this notion of quality time, invented no doubt by ambitious, career-minded mothers, is nonsense. Mothers have to be around when children want them, not when mothers have spare time. Postcards are a poor substitute for talk. How can she stand the guilt of all this? I wouldn't be able to.

But that's enough for now. I've stayed up late deliberately in the hope of sleeping soundly. I don't want to have bad dreams tonight. Last night I dreamed I was in a huge house, a house in England it must have been, climbing up endless flights of stairs which were piled high with obstacles of all sorts. I'd climb, panting, to the top of each pile, only to see another pile to be scaled. Eventually, in despair, I found myself teetering on a narrow platform which was somehow, in the way of dreams, strung between flights. It was like a swing bridge, swaying unpredictably. I was terrified. I jumped, and then I woke up. And didn't know what I had jumped into.

Irene has explained her addiction to letter-writing to her sons. 'You know I'm a dinosaur,' she has said more than once, 'your dreadfully old-fashioned mother who is intimidated by high-tech everything.' And the children know that their parents met in an Australian post office – it made them tolerant of their mother's haunting of the one in the village, her constant checking of the letterbox.

When Irene was eight her family moved to a township in rural Victoria. This meant separation from her grandfather, who had been the first man in her life. She began, then, to write to him about this new and fascinating place which he showed not the slightest desire to visit. She continued to write to him, and he to her, until his death sixteen years later. Every Wednesday morning during her student years, a square white envelope marked by crabbed handwriting would be waiting in the letter-board of her college.

When Irene's grandfather died, her mother, going through his things, found a very early letter of Irene's tucked into his wallet and immediately burst into tears. This little paper ghost, this evidence of love. Irene wanted her grandfather's letters to die along with him, disappear in a kind of spontaneous combustion, but she could not burn them herself. She still has many of them, and she is certain she has all of her mother's.

In Greece Irene kept all her letters; when none

came or when Hellenic or Australia Post went on strike, she would reread them. Letters are Irene's way of going for a walk, or dancing. They simply warm her and make her happy. But some letters, thinks Irene, are difficult to write; the receipt of others does not make her happy at all.

And there seems to be some sort of immutable law that the most longed-for letter never comes. Joachim does not write, but Irene does not blame him for this. It is not possible to force people to write, in spite of the baiting of any number of epistolary hooks. Even when your favourite person does write, you cannot expect him to say what you want to hear. A letter is a voice, after all.

I r e n e   I am unsure of most things. I know very little about anything. But I do know that love is stronger than death, stronger than separation. Because I love Joachim with my whole heart he is always with me. Perhaps the letters I am writing will be a bit of me to keep with him. I also know that if I shut my eyes there is no knowing where I am, and so, within seconds, I have left London behind and am with Joachim in the village.

There, right now, the leaves from the vines are starting to drift, yellow and brown, but much more slowly than they are here. Vines first, then the poplars. Bunches of grapes are hanging weightily, the smell of must is lingering in the lanes, and Vasili's sister will shortly make *mustalevriá*, that pudding made from must and tapioca and flour which the boys so adore, and which I have never learned to make. A veritable frenzy of blanket and rug-washing is upon the women, and they will be talking constantly of δουλειά, work, and how it never stops.

The pattern of the day has little variation. Every morning Petros the postman yells along the street, while here in Hampstead the clunk of the letterbox and the downward sigh of the letter is all that is ever heard. Village life is not quiet; the fishmonger's tape reiterates brassily: ψάρια, φρέσκα ψάρια, ψάρια Καλαμών. Fish, fresh fish, Kalamata fish. Tinkers and gypsies call in the lanes. It is not necessary to leave the village, for between them the shops and the gypsies sell everything. Gypsy wives push handcarts fitted out with racks of dangling dresses; their husbands drive vehicles loaded with plastic tables and chairs, or watermelon and cantaloupe, or chickens. Thomas and Michael bought two chickens once, long, long ago, and christened them David and Edward. What names are these? queried Yiayia.

In the evening the rose light bathes the mountains, and Joachim and his friends play basketball or football or practise their dancing, the *kalamatiano* or the *tsamiko*. Joachim is a pleasure to watch when he dances. Nimble, athletic, airborne, he moves so easily, but then he comes from a long line of good dancers.

At present Vasili, too, is away, but Joachim's favourite aunt and uncle are looking after him, wrapping him in uncritical, unconditional affection. They are always *there*. So are his cousins, and his cousin Pano's baby daughter staggers towards him, arms outstretched, whenever anybody says, Που είναι ο Ιωακείμ; – Where's Joachim? She grabs him round the knees and they flash toothy, delighted grins at each other.

Joachim goes across the road to visit his old, old yiayia, who is also always there. Sometimes she knows him, sometimes she doesn't, but he has the secret of arousing her from her apathy. He mentions olive oil, and how he is thinking of taking some of hers. Sparks to a tinder-box: she flares immediately. 'Aha! That's what *you* think, my fine fellow!'

In the second week of September school will start. Joachim may be glad that I will not be there to grumble about the teachers. He will have his name-day on the ninth of the month, and he will troop, he and his classmates, to church on September the fourteenth, which is Του Σταυρού, the Feast of the Exaltation of the Honourable and Life-giving Cross, one of the Twelve Great Feasts.

The Athenians have gone home, of course. It will be Easter before they come again, trailing clouds of sophistication, enjoying the return to their roots, lording it over the village children. Joachim and his peers are tolerant; they know they are the real thing. They live in the home of their ancestors, close to the land. They are not city-slickers.

Speaking of ancestors, I must remember to tell Joachim that among the tenacious farmer-priests are a couple of famous people. Cornish Richard Trevithick, inventor of the steam pump, is one; Australian H. V. McKay, inventor of the Sunshine Harvester, is another. I'll ask Joachim to please invent an olive-harvester that does everything. He'll laugh and say he wishes he could.

Now Irene, too, is in the home of her ancestors, or in one of them, here in England. She has been to Scotland only three times, and to Ireland not at all, an omission which she intends to rectify. She does not feel very much at home though, and occasionally thinks, now that she is in her fiftieth year, that she is not meant to feel at home anywhere. She did not have a home when she was born. Of course one was found, but it was only temporary, as were others, so that by the time she was thirteen she had lived in nine houses and six different towns.

Home, people think, is a place. This is most often true, but not always. Sometimes home is a person. When one soul recognises another, loneliness is annihilated, and comfort comes from a sense of belonging. Irene recognised a soul like that not so long ago, but in spite of all her efforts she has no home. Perhaps her efforts in this case were too timid, but she cannot be bold.

Here in Hampstead a light rain is falling through the yellowing lime trees but Irene is two thousand miles and twenty years away. Only thoughts of Joachim anchor her to the present.

I r e n e   Joachim takes for granted the fact that he has lived in only one house, the one that was built when I was expecting him. But after sixteen months of living in Yiayia's house and sleeping in a bed in the upstairs passage, Thomas said, 'You mean Michael and I are going to have a real room of our own, with a *door?'*

In the winter of 1975/6, home was very much on my mind.

December 1975

I hope all my mail has been arriving. I'm the post office's most constant customer. The man there thinks I'm demented. He charges me exorbitant rates for my postcards because I write more than a certain number of words on them, and then he covers most of what I've written with the most enormous stamps I've ever seen.

The man was Aristides. He's still there and he still thinks I'm demented, although after all this time he's fairly convinced I'm harmless. But the rules and regulations, the whole notion of control, were starting to get me down. So were other things. I want Joachim to understand all this. Whether he will or not is another matter.

Whenever the children and I go past the priest's house he is sure to be there, and always checks up on where we've been and where we're going.

Christmas Day was miserable in more ways than one. The weather was frightful: cold, wet, and generally dreary. I was in a sweat of nervous apprehension about Michael's impending christening at 4 p.m. Everybody nearly fainted with horror when I produced my knitting on Christmas Eve. That made me feel bad, and next day I wasn't even allowed to wash Michael's nappy! You can run yourself ragged preparing mountains of food, but you can't preserve the basic rules of hygiene! Christmas dinner was eaten in my absence, and everybody started to get disorganised (in the usual fashion) for the christening party.

After watching a funeral procession from

behind the kitchen curtains I decided I wanted
to be buried at sea.

Joachim will definitely not understand that reaction:
Orthodox funerals, and he has been to quite a few, are
the only ones he knows.

It was all very difficult, and not helped by the fact
that his brothers were accident-prone.

Round about this time we had a rash of small
accidents. Thomas somehow poked a
pomegranate seed up his nose. I panicked, of
course, but managed to get it out. Shortly
afterwards he was kicked in the stomach by
the donkey, but is determined to learn the
hard way, because he still gets too close to said
animal's hind legs. While holding Michael one
afternoon I fell three or four steps down into
the courtyard and landed on top of his right
leg. Needless to say, I immediately burst into
tears, mainly from fright over Michael's leg.
He was roaring and Thomas immediately
became hysterical because I was crying. Vasili
and Yiayia were both out and I didn't have a
clue where they were. However, we soon
recovered, and Michael's leg is still in working
order.

A couple of days later, Thomas went into

the yard with the chooks and fell heavily on
the concrete. I was in the throes of rescuing
him when the blasted white rooster took two
savage pecks at me. Fortunately I was wearing
trousers, so my leg is still intact. I've told
Yiayia that that bird is next for the chopper.
The turkey went the way of all poultry flesh
on Christmas Eve, by the way. Yiayia does the
slaughtering – wrings their necks. Ugh.

Shortly after this, Thomas leaned over the courtyard wall and said, 'Where's the rooster, Yiayia?' The
rooster had indeed been eaten for his sins.

Once again I have rescued Thomas from the
yard. Another fall on the concrete and another
lump on the head. There is always someone
crying. Michael has fallen two or three steps a
couple of times, but won't learn.

I didn't learn, either, incurable romantic that I am.
And Vasili, at least where home and mother were
concerned, was worse than I. Joachim has learned that
much.

January 1976

We are very reluctant to return home, I'm
afraid, in spite of continuing difficulties with

our offspring. We spend our spare time
dreaming up get-rich-quick schemes so that
we can come again. Vasili is not at all
disappointed in Greece and would be happy
to stay. Enough said.

A child cannot be expected to know, or to understand, what has gone before. His parents are merely
that; it takes a long time for them to become people,
individuals, and the most difficult thing of all is to
imagine one's parents as lovers. I think it impossible,
actually. Will Joachim ever know how very much I
loved his father, how much I wanted Vasili to be
happy?

I want Joachim to know all sorts of things, so I'm
doing my best to paint a pale wash of the past as a
background to his present. In yet another way his
brothers have done this, too. They did the spade-
work, to change the metaphor. They prepared the way
for him, made the road as straight as they could.

Suddenly my thoughts turn to Juliet, as they so
often do, to Juliet with her only child; Juliet with her
good sense, her fortitude, her practicality. I wonder
whether I could have left a daughter and an only child?
Very probably not, so I would have gone quietly mad
instead, mad from grief and disillusionment once I discovered that I did not know Vasili at all, and that he
had never really cared about me; when I saw the

pointlessness of living in a world where people hoarded and fed and slept and knew not me. I do not imagine that a child would have saved me in the long run, although Joachim certainly did once – got me through a summer that seemed to last a hundred years.

I envy Juliet for all sorts of reasons. I envy her because of the clear break with her past. She came to Greece, met Pavlos and married him. England represents her old, single life; Greece her new, married life. There are no clear divisions in my life. The outlines have always been blurred, by questions, by assumptions of impermanence. Will we stay? Will we go? When? Where? This is the way it is always going to be, I fear.

Juliet loves Greece – yes, she does – but it is hard to know whether she and I love it in the same way, hard to know whether she feels wrenched by thoughts of England. Juliet never looks back. At least I don't think she does.

⊡⊡

Attachments are Irene's problem. One of her problems. People stalk her dreams by night, and by restless day. Her dead grandparents, her dead mother, her children, their father. Artemis. Juliet. Joachim. It seems to her that she dreams about Joachim every night. But there is one attachment she never talks about. She will make oblique reference to it in her letters to Joachim, as part of an explanation of love in general, but will provide no details, even though she remembers each detail, no matter how small, and the memory hurts whenever she touches it, which is all too often. She cannot forget.

Irene has an attachment to a reality that has vanished. A manila folder of old photographs is part of her luggage, along with the letters and the notebooks, as if she has to have visible evidence of a life lived for fifty years. It should be recorded that she even has a photograph of herself as a baby: cheerful, bright-eyed, with toes peeping out from under a cream smocked dress and hands outstretched to the world. There are a couple of graduation photos, photos of her own babies, but now, and this fact must be significant, it is the older photographs that she turns to most regularly.

In one of these, Irene's mother stands in a wedding dress of georgette, a mist of tulle veil reaching past the huge bouquet and satin-covered horseshoe which did not bring her as much luck as she deserved. Irene's father is in uniform. He clutches his glengarry; his jacket bristles with sunburst badges and their three scrolls. His free hand holds his bride's gloved one. He is also wearing a proud smile: look what I've got. He didn't know, actually, what he had got. Most men never do, thinks Irene.

Briefly she considers Pavlos, Juliet's husband. Does Pavlos realise what he has in Juliet? Why are some men so careless? Why is their vanity so complete, their imagination so vestigial, that they expect women to put up with everything and still adore them? A mystery. But then men are a mystery: *terra incognita*.

Irene returns to thoughts of her mother and her mother's attributes: beauty, courage, fortitude, wit, intelligence, grace, charm. The list could easily be added to. Gone, all gone, thinks Irene, although she cannot believe it. She never will.

The surprise-packet of marriage, ponders Irene further. Neither person is what the other expects. Irene is not like her mother; her mother did not desert her children, would never have contemplated such drastic action. She was happy. Irene chops at these thoughts the moment they appear and turns to a still older photograph, that of her grandfather, the first man in her life, the person to whom she started writing when she was eight. He rescued his daughter-in-law and new granddaughter when they had no home to go to and took them to live in country Victoria until his son came home from the war. Irene's grandfather was half Scottish, half Cornish. He was fair and very slight and shy and diffident. He was, above all, a gentle man, and Irene loved him with all her heart.

I r e n e   Perhaps I should post this photograph of my grandfather to Joachim, although he might not be at all interested in this ancient ancestor and the differences between their lives. The sepia is fading slightly and the paper is speckling round the edges: it was taken in 1900. It is too valuable, really, to risk posting – a description will have to do for the time being. A sort of picture history. I'll describe others, too, while I'm at it, others I remember well even though they are on shelves and in boxes on the other side of the world. Might as well give him the works. After all, he knows all about the Greek side of the family.

In the photograph from 1900 a child of seven, lips turned up slightly at the corners, stares confidently at the camera. A lace collar spreads over the shoulders of his Norfolk jacket, his knickerbockers are buttoned below the knee, and black stockings fill the gap between his trousers and his high button-up boots. One hand rests lightly on his belt, the other holds a model sailing ship in full rig.

The child's early life was one of ease and comfort. He lived in a township near the Murray River, and home was a hotel which he shared with his parents, five siblings, and a small army of servants. When one of the latter suggested that the child might like to clean his own boots, my grandfather was genuinely amazed. 'I? But I'm the publican's son.'

He was also the mine-owner's son, for Great-grandfather combined several careers. Every week, when the gold came in, Great-grandfather gave his eldest son half a crown, fishing the coin out of a waist-coat pocket. The waistcoat had several pockets, for a gold-chased matchbox resided in one, and a gold fob-watch in another. A small nugget dangled from the watch-chain. Father and son had their weekly appointment, but not much else apparently, for Great-grandfather was much more interested in horses, dogs, football, cricket, wine, women and song than in mere children, who were easily got and almost as easily ignored.

Time wore on for my grandfather, with routine a surface layer concealing change, much as the ticking of his fob-watch and the slow movement of its hands were the only outward signs of the steady activity of wheels, cogs and sprockets hidden beneath the thin layer of gold. He sat on a long wooden form in the one-teacher school, droning his tables, reciting the rivers of Victoria: Murray, Goulburn, Campaspe, Loddon, Kiewa, Buckland, Ovens – a long list – and pushing a steel nib which sputtered and blotted on rough lined paper. Two rows across sat my grandmother, two years younger, watching and waiting as she would do at other times and in other places, until 1919 when they married.

West of the school and township, again near the Murray, my other grandfather, the one I never knew, already fifteen, ploughed paddocks and also watched and waited for the future, never dreaming of the drought and flood which would ruin his family and drive him off the land forever. I have no picture of him.

In 1900 my grandfather started violin lessons. He clattered out of the house twice a week, carefully carrying the honey-coloured instrument which I would learn to play, badly, sixty years later. It was wrapped in a yellow silk scarf and nestled in red velvet inside a case which was wooden-ridged and coffin-shaped and nearly as big as he was. On his return, his hand traced the smoothly curving banister and his feet sank into soft carpet as he climbed the stairs to bed. His mother sat embroidering by gaslight. Some evenings the tinkle of the piano and snatches of songs sung by tenors and light baritones floated upwards: *Speak to Me, Thora; The Harp that Once thro' Tara's Halls.* He sped to magic lantern shows, to football and cricket matches, and stepped sedately to church every Sunday morning. In 1900 you knew where you were.

In 1910 things were different: one of the pictures I remember is very large. In the fast-falling dusk of the Edwardian age, the huge wealthy family of three generations assembles on the lawn in front of a Rive-rina mansion. My grandfather, aged seventeen, is cele-brating his grandparents' golden wedding anniversary. Now tall enough to be in the back row, he stares solemnly at the camera. But his mouth is straight and there is a tense set to his head, with the light hair brushed across a high brow. Standing with his uncles, he is only one in a long row of white collars and dark jackets. In front sit the corseted matrons, and on the manicured grass there is a tumble of lace, ribbons and ringlets where the little girls are kneeling.

In that year of 1910 my grandfather was a junior teacher and not showing much promise. The gold had started to peter out. So had the hotel trade, for much of its money used to come in even before breakfast as the miners changed shifts. The hotel burned down and was uninsured.

But a pattern persisted for a little longer. Tennis, football, church socials, violin competitions all continued, in spite of my grandfather moving away from home in order to take charge of a tiny school. In August 1914 he wondered and waited to see what would happen. Would it all be over by Christmas? It would not, but still he lingered, did not change his life, say goodbye to youth, until 1915. By 1915, I have been told, Joachim's Greek great-uncle had survived the second Balkan war and a period in a Bulgarian prison camp. But he had no youth at all, and was dead by 1920.

I flip the pages of the photo album in my mind and create an effect like film: big guns jerk to scenes of mud, bare trees, shadows of armed men, coils of barbed wire, and then to my grandfather, grinning lopsidedly under a slouch hat and drunk with fatigue, French wine and rum.

After four years of fear, terror, mud, slush, depriva-
tion and disillusionment, he came home from the
war – unutterably weary but looking forward to the
future. The homecoming was not without its difficulties. Arriving unexpectedly, he discovered his fiancée,
my grandmother, playing the piano and singing for
another man. He also discovered that he owned only
his uniform, for his mother had given his civilian
clothes and his army pay to his brothers. But the wedding took place and off they went, my grandparents, to
another one-teacher school further south, to a cottage
which had a separate kitchen with a clay floor, a vegetable garden and chooks scratching in the dirt.

There are two photographs from this period. One
is of the general store on mail day: children sit on
horses, waiting, while adults sit in jinkers and gigs, also
waiting – for letters. Letters, crossed and recrossed in
spidery writing, that have taken months to come from
Britain and weeks to come from other parts of Australia. My grandmother receives an annual plea from
the township on the Murray. 'Come home for
Christmas, Doris, I entreat you, for it will be my last!'
My grandmother sees twenty of her mother's last
Christmases, all in all.

The second photograph is of the school: the
corrugated-iron roof on which rain beats all too seldom, chimneys topped by little tin hats, ridges of
weatherboard on walls, rungs on water tanks, gum

trees and low hills behind the building, and thirty-one children in front. They stand to attention, every one, and the camera has caught the flutter of their skirts and jackets, frozen forever in the autumn breeze of 1921. Their faces are slightly blurred, as the past must be, preserving an outline rather than individual features.

The pictures multiply during the next forty-five years. Other houses, other schools, towns, suburbs and gardens fall into place beside snapshots (language changes, too) of siblings, children, cousins, nephews, nieces, ageing parents, and other soldiers, other wars. Pictures of graduations, bowls presentations, church choirs, the Moderator of the Presbyterian Church, beaches, holidays, Sunday School concerts and picnics, dogs, farms, interstate capitals all lie in a big box and I shuffle them endlessly, finding new ones all the time, and discovering postcards of Piccadilly Circus and Glasgow inscribed 'With Love from Arthur' tucked away at the bottom. Magic names, magic places seize me, and I sit absorbing scenes which no longer exist and which I fear I will never see. My grandmother certainly never saw them.

A child of 1949 gazes up at me from the box – a serious, even solemn, child seated on a tricycle. A furry bear, Bozo, sits in front, and I wonder where he is now. He has gone, as has that child of four who sits gravely facing events to come. But if I look closely I can see the embroidery on Bozo's braces and the shadow of a dimple in the child's cheek. For I felt, as my grand-father had felt nearly fifty years before, that living, although a serious business, had its lighter side.

Twenty years later, after a funeral, my aunt gave me a colour print. 'Just a keepsake,' she said constrictedly. 'We think it's the last one.'

I can hardly bear to look at it, but I do, and see an old man in a boat. He is leaning forward, fussing slightly over his fishing-rod; a wreath of smoke drifts upward and every grain in his tweedy cap is visible, for technology has raced away in seventy years. This time he is looking away from the camera and I find the change significant. Now nobody knows what he sees.

Yes, I'll write something like this to Joachim. He looks a little like his great-grandfather. I must remember to tell him that.

In the past Irene studied and taught history. Sometimes she wishes she had been a scientist or mathematician, but some things cannot be altered and at least her historian's training makes her think about the pattern of the past. Her view of the past, of life, has changed. Once she thought of life as a progress along a con-tinuum. The detours and T-junctions were merely incidental, minor delays along the track. Now she understands – and with what bitterness – that life is a drama, and not necessarily a well-made play at that.

She wonders about the distinctions between the new world and the old, between the nomads and the settlers. Pioneers anticipate change and development; peasants expect everything to remain the same. It makes for security and certainty, that expectation. For some people hardship seems preferable to the risk of the new. Change hurts.

The historian in Irene appreciates Greece, loves the thought of the long thread of time unravelling. It is a visible thread, too, whereas the lines and threads in Australia seem, at least to expatriate Irene, visible only to the Aboriginal people.

I r e n e   I will tell Joachim that in January 1976 we four – Vasili, Thomas, Michael and I – made our first trip to the Mani, that land of rock and scattered olive trees, of bare mountains and intricate networks of stone fences. We visited a convent that had been built in 1769. I compared the dates immediately and described the place to my mother.

January 1976

The convent of the order of Evangelismos is small and rather haphazard in design, with a carefully tended garden. The gate is a crimson cross-inscribed door with foliage hanging down over it. A tiny little nun came with us into the chapel and showed us the minute original chapel and the date painted inside the sanctuary. Vasili asked how many nuns there were and she replied, 'As many as you see.' What a life.

But that is the life some people choose.

Three days later we were off again, this time to Pylos, where Thomas and Michael, naturally enough, were more interested in a boat trip on the Bay of Navarino than in the architecture and history of the brooding Neokastro. I have never told Joachim that he visited Pylos in 1981, before he was born. Oh, Mu-um, I hear him say, who wants to know that?

He might know already, though, that Greece is the place for synchronicities. Once again I wrote to my mother.

January 1976

We met an older Australian couple in the Pylos bus. They are schoolteachers from Kew. She teaches near Reservoir where there are a lot of migrants, hence her interest in Modern Greek. They were going to Chora to see Nestor's Palace, were in the bus on the way back and had also had a lovely day.

I did not find out their names until years later. Mary had already visited us, in 1987, and still we did not realise we had met before, until she, back in Melbourne, started going through old slides and diary entries and came across an entry about a Greek-Australian couple with two little boys. On her next visit, in 1989, she walked into the post office at Andritsaina, seventy kilometres from the village, and told the employee there that she wanted to telephone Vasili in the village.

'I'm his first cousin,' beamed the man. 'He's not on the phone, but I'll drive you there.' And Joachim's Uncle Panayioti, greatly excited, delivered Mary to the door.

Such things happen in Greece. Last summer Joachim and I agreed that the only thing one can expect in Greece is to be surprised. We laughed; he wrote the thought down for me, and the piece of paper is here now as I sit writing in this house in Hampstead. The tablecloth is blue and white and so are the coffee mugs: the precise blue of the Greek flag. They are not mine, these things, but symbols of Greece confront me wherever I go. And sometimes wound me . . . There are even two fig trees in the back garden, vastly inferior specimens to Yiayia's two. But then the poplar here is a giant, not like the slim ones of the Peloponnese.

There is a constant grinding of layers, of dimensions, of I don't know what. Whereas in Greece I read

English compulsively in order to hear its voices at least in my head, here in Hampstead I wax neurotic over the state of my Greek and make trips to Queensway in order to buy *To Vyma*. At monstrous expense, of course. There must be Greek newspapers closer to hand but I do not, as yet, know London very well. I have even, I blush to confess, spoken to a total stranger, a Greek man, in a supermarket. I'll tell Joachim, but not Vasili; he'd be mortified. The thing is, I miss the sound of Greek. I miss speaking it, too. Strange, that; I never thought I would. The graft did take, after all.

That makes my present situation difficult. What an understatement! I have spent nearly thirty years in a Greek world and nearly fifteen years in Greece itself. I cannot say goodbye, but neither could I stay and struggle on.

People do not seem to understand this. I don't think Juliet does, for example, although we have never discussed my leaving. I have avoided the subject and she is too well-mannered to probe deeply. But I suspect she thinks I should try again. Does she, loving Pavlos as she does, have any knowledge or understanding of aversion, antipathy, dislike? It is a sad thing, negative emotion, and people prefer not to think about it.

Give it another go, people say. Save the marriage, salvage something. Think of your children. You're a strong woman, you can do it. But I'm not and I can't. At this point, after so long, my will is not involved: it has come to this.

One man, clearly a good Christian, instructed me to treat Vasili and his mother as I would like to be treated. It works, he said. Do unto others. I was amazed at the time that he did not hear me scream, and even more amazed that I managed to keep such a loud noise safely under lock and key, imprisoned somewhere between diaphragm and vocal cords.

But the words formed perfectly, even if they did not escape. Go over there and try it yourself. See where it gets you. I tried it for years and years, and all I ever heard was the purr of the predator, all I ever saw was the smile of the tiger.

A r t e m i s　　I am not sure what time it is. Early evening, possibly, as the family is here. What's left of it. There is the usual noise of conversation around me, words drifting. I am snatching at one or two. Somebody mentions Australia: there is a word I can hold and think on, for I went to that place once.

My son wanted me to go: that is a thought I have had before. So I went, but could never have stayed: that thought I have also had before, many, many times. It was necessary to be home for Easter. To be away from home at Easter-time is unthinkable, always. In any case, what I was doing, even for a short time, in that foreign place with its upside-down seasons, buzzing flies and tasteless food?

What my son ever saw in it I do not know. I suppose he only stayed as long as he did because of his foreign wife. But he could have had any woman he wanted here at home. Why did he not choose the known way? The unexpected falls into every life; we should not go to meet it, should not invite it in. A great many people do, of course. I see that now. But παλιά, way back then, poverty forced them to do this. The unexpected is bad, but poverty is worse.

I met all the homesick villagers there in that big Australian city, the name of which I forget. The name doesn't matter. It's foreign and surely all big cities are much the same, except for our Αθήνα. But the names of the villagers come back to me across the oceans, and across an ocean of time as well. Thothoro, Petro, Panayioti, Thanassi, Angelo, and all the rest with their wives from our mountain villages. Go back, I remember saying to them. Think of your mothers, your village. Go back. It is there you should be – at home. But they shook their heads sadly. It is too late, they said, we have been here too long.

I understood. The foreign wife did not. Not then, not ever. I see her now in the eye of my mind. I see her as she was: smiling, young, very foolish. 'It is never too late,' she said, not just once. And, 'Never say never.' The stupidity of her. In a sense, it is always too late, for as soon as we are born we begin to die. And the pattern is set for us before we are born, give or take a few individual strands which seem to be woven despite our efforts, like the errors and faults which are a mark of anything handmade. To attempt to weave your own pattern is certain folly.

New fashions, different things, foreign people, are always dangerous. Always. Fate must not be tempted. Nor is it good to strive for happiness, for the Evil Eye is drawn to happiness and beauty and tries to destroy both. Caution is the best thing, is always necessary. On the rare occasions I admire my grandchildren, and Joachim is the one I admire most often, I take great care to spit, *Phtou! Phtou!* I drive the Eye away, I cloud its vision.

Here in the village our way of life stretches back into the past forever, longer than anybody can remember. I knew and remember, with an effort, the foreigner's parents, but knew nothing, and can never know anything, of their parents. Here in the village the memory of grandparents, even of ancestors long-gone, is passed on, so that people alive today know what to expect. What could we hope to know of the foreigner? What little we could know was almost certainly the wrong thing, different from our way. How could she leave her own? That alone was cause for suspicion. People are not meant to live apart, away from the lives they know, away from their own places. Even the villagers who live in Athens keep coming back, as is natural and right. One place for everybody. Surely it is impossible to love, to belong to, more than one?

And now my thoughts are wandering. I can never control them for long. Words refuse to join up in my head. They, the family, are holding the mirror in front of my face. I look once, and then close my eyes.

J u l i e t Night time. Diary time. Joanna is asleep. Pavlos is out. If I'm still up and writing when he comes in he'll assume that I'm preparing or correcting for school. He never really asks what I'm doing and these days I'm glad about this, although I used to want him to show some interest in my interests; wanted, I suppose, a companion. But you can't expect companionship from men. I told Irene that once. She glared at me and said in her stubborn way, 'Well, if I can't have companionship from men, and I agree that I can't, then I'd rather be on my own.' I didn't take much notice at the time, but of course she meant it. That is the difference, or one of the differences, between us. I would *not* rather be on my own.

I've been thinking a lot about what migration

means – about how it demands using a part of yourself you've never used before. And how often when an unused part gets exercised the result is torn muscles, pain and exhaustion. Sometimes a recovery takes place, sometimes it doesn't.

And then there's the matter of the essential self. Our essential selves get lost, I think, but sometimes it's better not to find them, better to acknowledge the fact that migration is a kind of death – death of the old self. Perhaps this is the way it has to be for any migration to be even moderately successful. This was one of Irene's problems, at least I think so. Her old self never quite died, and she could not kill it off.

Now something is driving her, something inexorable, irresistible, and that something is almost certainly her old self. She couldn't consent to its execution, but she ignored it for far too long and for all the wrong reasons. That's asking for trouble. Her old self, at some stage, and for some reason, started to breathe again and to become demanding. It seems to me that she plugged her ears against its siren's song for as long as she could, until it came wailing in regardless.

Then again, Irene just isn't the type to live in a Greek village. For all sorts of reasons, really. She was unfortunate in her family pattern, in her very Australianness. I met her parents once. Nice people, full of the milk of human kindness, but quite hopelessly naïve, as Australians, older ones at least, so often are.

Generous. Talkative. Letting it all hang out. I'm not sure about the present generation. Even I, cut off from modern trends, know that Australia is an ever-changing place and now quite unrecognisable, say, to my parents. Irene, born just at the end of the war, is fond of saying that her generation of Australians is the last of its kind. She's probably right, and it's probably just as well.

These parents of hers married young, as she did; they believed absolutely in the brotherhood of man and socialist ideals. What hope did their daughter have? Naïveté is only attractive in the young, I told her once when particularly fed up. She takes these things from me, but then she takes a great deal from everybody. I've seen the look of surprised pain in her eyes often. I waited and waited for a reaction, because I wanted her to exert herself, to *grow up*, but after the initial flash the pain was always buried very deep.

The Australians I've observed are often very surprised when people aren't *nice*. It takes them quite a long time to realise that many Europeans are suspicious of warmth. It is a theory of mine that the nature of a culture has a lot to do with the way in which that culture organises its space. Here in Europe, space is carved up into smaller spaces and complicated by various types of wall: high hedgerows, fences of every sort. In Greece prickly pear is often used as a type of fence. I've seen many photographs of the Australian countryside, and the ones I remember are of vast areas lying fallow or under wheat, plains dotted with trees and the occasional windmill. Strands of wire enclose enormous fields. Paddocks, they call them. Australians simplify space, and then they get lost in that threatening place the bush, because it's so dense and complicated, or so I've been told. Europeans are used to complicated space and they often make it more complicated.

As for temperament, an outlook, a way of doing things, whatever you like to call it, Australians in Europe think, initially anyway, that openness will get them everywhere. In fact it gets them nowhere, for European wiliness regards it as foolishness, simplicity. In this way, Irene is very Australian. She was, is, far too honest and open for her own good. Trusting. Innocent. People took advantage of her, and when she realised that this had happened, and she didn't always, she was deeply hurt. They owed her money, cheated her, broke promises, lied to her, ordered her about, humiliated her in public, and generally tried to break her spirit. She was prepared to be hurt, as any migrant, as any adult, has to be but everyone has a limit, and she reached hers. Perhaps worse than all these things was the indifference: I think she felt they didn't care. In a sense she had to learn to see and recognise cruelty. When she finally learned to do this, the end was already very near. Or perhaps it was that the end was ensured once she had learned.

Until then, though, she was like a modern Lady of

Shalott. How did the poem go? 'She knows not what the curse may be/And so she weaveth steadily'. Irene was always busy, frantically busy. In the poem it was the sight of Sir Lancelot in the mirror that did the damage. But Irene had had a vision of Sir Lancelot long, long before; the curse which came upon her was an awakening to reality which happened very late, and which she did not want.

He sang, 'Tirra Lirra,' by the river, Sir Lancelot, but Irene understood, far too late as I've said, that in spite of his physical splendour and his dazzling setting, he hadn't been singing for her. His song was one she could listen to, for its melody enchanted her, but its words were ones she would never learn. In one way, I can't blame her for leaving, because it all comes back to me now: I remember what happened to the Lady of Shalott.

Once Irene the nomad had put childhood and her student days and her early married life behind her she began to travel again; so far she has not stopped travelling for very long. Her mother-in-law was always critical of this desire to escape; her friend Juliet was inclined to be envious but thought it, on the whole, not a good thing. So unsettling. Exactly, thought Irene. Exactly. Who wants to settle?

Joachim is very well travelled but complains to

Irene that he can remember little of his numerous journeys. By the time he was four he had visited Germany, Luxembourg, Italy, Turkey and Australia. Vasili and Irene took turns at the pusher, sharing walks of eight or ten kilometres a day, while Thomas and Michael trotted alongside, not always placidly. On board a ferry Joachim gazed in bewilderment after a toy car as it fell into the deep, deep Adriatic where he had thrown it. Irene well remembers the look on his face.

Since then Joachim has been to Crete, to England and to Australia three more times. This probably means, thinks Irene, that he will long for a very settled life: carpet slippers, armchair, newspaper, coffee and worry beads.

I r e n e   We four, I will tell Joachim, came to Greece again at the end of 1977, arriving safely after a nightmare journey. Michael, then aged three, split his trousers even before we boarded the plane in Melbourne, an ill omen surely. Delays in Singapore, Bombay and Beirut followed. Both boys had to have cholera injections in Singapore, and Thomas went on a hunger-strike yet again, which seems hard to believe now.

In order to distract ourselves in Singapore, we went to a tourist concert called the Instant-Asia Cultural Show, and Michael disgraced himself by shaking with fright from start to finish. Chinese fan dancers and Hindu beauties with tinkling bells held no charms for him at all. When the 'lion' did its traditional dance of welcome he screamed blue murder and Vasili had to carry him out. Family honour was restored to a certain degree when Thomas, who was only five then, volunteered to have the snake-charmer's huge python draped round his neck. The audience was most impressed, Vasili felt ill with terror, and I, as usual, went completely numb. Of course we knew the python's fangs had been removed, but it made little difference.

At Bombay airport, after Thomas, Michael and I had exhausted the possibilities of the short row of shops, we went into a tiny cinema to view the documentaries being screened. We made a hasty exit when film of bodies floating down the Ganges began to roll. At Beirut airport a young soldier, armed to the teeth, seized Thomas and bolted with him up a flight of stairs while Vasili and I goggled and gasped in dismay. It was the soldier's idea of a joke and was all over very quickly, before the volatile Thomas even had a chance to react. That was something to be thankful for, at least. But Vasili, not unnaturally, had had enough: at one stage of the journey he gloomily remarked that the aeroplane was so awful that even the travel-sickness bags were second-hand.

Michael was not even reassured by our arrival in

Athens. At the Tomb of the Unknown Warrior in Syntagma Square he loved the pigeons and hated the evzones, screeching loudly if we went too close to one. In the National Gardens he saw a giant lurking behind every tree and kept begging to be taken back to the hotel. Joachim will find this hard to believe: his big soldier brother.

The plane which took us south to the Peloponnese was a two-engined machine and did not inspire confidence. I swore I could hear it changing gear. Even before we left Athens Vasili heard the pilot ask a technician, 'Who serviced this thing?' A name was mentioned. '*He* did?' spat the pilot disgustedly. 'He couldn't even take out his own eyes!'

But we arrived safely and were pampered and made much of. The olive harvest took place in freezing cold. There were a few variations. Vasili had sent the money for a shower to be installed, and there it was – a telephone arrangement and a plastic bowl. Michael hated it. He hated nearly everything: three seems to be a difficult age. I wrote to my mother, as usual.

December 1977

Since arriving in the village Michael has been
conducting a campaign of passive resistance.
He refuses to speak Greek to anyone, and is
only speaking to me. This line of action is
making us both popular, of course. Everybody

keeps remarking on how different he is from Thomas.

Michael would stand on the threshold of the kitchen and exhort me not to speak Greek. This effort he kept up for ten days and then caved in completely, beginning to speak a rapid and grammatical Greek with great ease, much to Vasili's surprise.

Bright days abounded, I recall, even in deep December. We visited Koroni, later one of my favourite places. It is so like a postcard with its blue and white houses, with carnations, ivy geraniums and roses spilling over walls, and the best view in the world framed by the entrance to the castle. It was there, later, that Vasili told my Australian Great-uncle Pat, of whom Joachim is so fond, about the bishop whose enemies had thrown him over the ramparts.

'H'm,' said Pat, looking down, 'that wouldn't have done him a lot of good.'

Years later, Joachim and Vasili went fishing on the Koroni waterfront, and nearly every little boy in the town joined them. And I, I found a sulphur-crested cockatoo. There he was, caged near a house built within the castle walls.

'G'day,' I said, quite unable to speak Greek on this momentous occasion. 'You're a long way from home.' And he looked at me knowingly out of his beady eyes. Yes, he did. I swear it. Way back then I wrote:

The day in Koroni. The drive there is quite
spectacular, as for much of the way the road
follows the sea while snow-capped mountains
are visible on the other side of the bay. In the
town several houses are within the castle
walls, and people run clotheslines between
thirteenth-century stones and keep pigeons in
old arrow-slits. Twenty nuns live in a convent
up there. An old nun gave Thomas and
Michael a badge each: Christ holding a plate
on which reposes the head of John the
Baptist.

I might tell you that Thomas is having
nightmares about the various maudlin bits of
religiosity that surround one here. The other
night he dreamed he was 'Christ with prickles
in his head'. One of Yiayia's icons was
responsible for that. So far we haven't had any
dreams about the real live (dead?) skeleton
which was hanging in one part of the convent.
Upon inquiry, it appeared that it is not a relic
of anyone famous but simply hangs there as a
lesson to us all: namely that life is short and
we all wind up thus. A note on a verse pinned
to its grisly form said as much. No beating
about the bush, burning or otherwise. You get
your religion straight in Greece.

I must ask Joachim whether he would have spoken to the cockatoo in Greek or English. Even though I miss the sound of Greek and even miss speaking it, I have never really changed my language. I have learned that to change your language you have to change your life, and, in the end, I found I couldn't do it, that I hadn't changed my life in essence. And without my mother tongue I felt orphaned: in Greek there was no answering echo.

In England there is at least for Irene a dialogue, rather than the monologue that went on for so long. The silence has been broken. And yet it is not as simple as that; even here she does not feel at home, does not feel that she communicates, does not fit in.

By Greek and Australian standards Irene is reserved, quiet. Here she often appears to be too open, too exuberant, in the habit of wearing her heart on her sleeve and far too inclined to that artlessness which is a feature of the colonial mentality and which the old powers consider so crass. But Australians, thinks Irene, have had to be like that: they could not rely on the demarcation of a class structure, did not know, in more ways than one, exactly where they were or who they were. They had to trust everyone, to depend on a great many, and they suffered for it.

In the end Irene could only be what she is: a slow learner. It took her a long time to realise that fate is a rat rather than an eagle. Fate comes creeping, slowly and surely it gnawed away at the rope of her life until the last thread snapped. And then there were consequences, and blame and sorrow and anger, all those things.

Irene hopes that Joachim does not blame anyone, that he takes the view that some things merely happen. But she does not know exactly what is in his heart and mind, does not know what he thinks in the drifting moments before sleep. He does not want to answer questions. When Irene asks them he flashes the smile that so wrenches her heart and says, 'I dunno.' He is right: it is better not to know. Irene wishes she did not know about certain matters.

She is muddled about the village. She does not want to stay there any more, but she does not want to leave it either. Thomas and Michael sense her deep confusion and sigh with exasperation. They may even be slightly jealous of Joachim, feeling that she grieves more for him than she does for them. But Joachim is so young. Then, too, he was the child of renewed hope, the symbol of a new beginning. When she thinks of these things Irene feels as if she knows all about shotgun blasts, for there is a gaping hole where her heart was, and every little nerve-end fringing that hole is ragged and raw.

I r e n e   Rilke wrote, 'Whoever is alone now will go on being alone, will stay up late, read, write long letters.' People who are alone also wander the streets, as I am wandering them now – taking in sights that might entertain Joachim. If I do this, I might be able to stop thinking. I am slowly tuning in, as it were, to life here, after being in neutral gear or on automatic pilot for days since leaving him.

In London, as in Melbourne, the sun can be shining and then rain suddenly fall even before the sun disappears: silvery, silken showers followed very shortly by pale blue sky again. In Hampstead, leaves are falling fast and men in yellow vests are busily sweeping up great drifts of them. When it rains the wide leaves run and drip in the way that olive branches cannot.

It is well and truly autumn now and the wet leaves make pavements treacherous and mere walking hazardous. Chestnuts, all spiky, litter the ground. One more sign of age: I take short steps and all care in the streets, afraid of slipping, haunted by thoughts of osteoporosis and the possibility of falling flat on my face – although a broken nose might offer a vague chance of improvement!

Life here, for me, is a little bland, a little muted, but blessedly anonymous. London itself is extremely varied, in the way that Australia, that multicultural nation, is varied. Beautiful black girls with shiny, skinny plaits go swinging up the High Street, or teeter along in very high heels. Pale, unlined Englishwomen of a certain age, status and income gaze in the boutique windows, and on Sunday afternoons there is almost shoulder-to-shoulder browsing in the local bookshops. Readers are kindly requested not to handle books while wearing gloves. I have never seen a notice like that before. All these minute differences that in a split second have the capacity to make the familiar strange.

Joachim would like the sight of the mounted police, their horses stepping sedately down the road, adjusting their pace to the slope: all that shine, gleam and ripple, the precision of presentation. Disciplined dogs on leashes may go virtually anywhere; our Toby would be sadly out of place, I fear, would not know how to behave at all.

The English and their pets. Inside a certain front fence a plaque has been erected to the memory of one Marmaduke, a hamster who used to go to work with his master, I am told, in the car. Once I saw a man with a dog in a pusher: owner wheeled pet onto the tube at Camden Town. If Vasili had been there it would have been another opportunity for him to look incredulous and stern at the same time.

I had enough occasions to look incredulous in the village. All those visits to Vasili's relatives, for example, those long intervals of sitting on straight-backed chairs while wind whistled in great draughts through gaping cracks, while window-panes shook slightly in the occasional earth tremor, and hosts and hostesses did their smiling duty, giving us everything they had. The houses often consisted of only two rooms. Streamers of onions and garlic hung from the kitchen rafters, yards of sausage were suspended from hooks inside the chimney, and kittens played under beds. Sheep were occasionally housed in the basement and then the stink of urine rose between the floorboards, mingling with smoke and the sharp smell of *pastó* and retsina.

Once I cast my gaze out a window to see Vasili's cousin's wife grab a rooster in one swift movement and in another deftly break its neck. She disappeared and less than two hours later, pieces of boiled chicken appeared on the table. Joachim doesn't visit places like this; they are disappearing fast, as roads, towns, television, cars and tourists all wreak change on a way of life.

It is only high in the mountain villages that things remain the same: a few of the old people are still there, with all their dignity, courtesy, their certainties and seductive simplicities. Joachim will recall that our friend June, on holiday from Australia, and I walked during the summer to the upper village where his Greek grandfather was born. It was not the first time we had done this, and the old people thought us lunatics or liars or both, for it is a twelve-kilometre walk and people there walk only for a reason, usually connected with work. But on our return from our first visit, dear Uncle Stavros was vastly entertained, clapped me on the back and chuckled and chortled while urging me to walk further next time.

This summer Joachim did not want to come. It's too hot, he said, and it'll be boring. Hot it certainly was, but it is never boring. June and I climbed and climbed a stone path worn smooth by time and donkeys' hooves, and stopped every so often to see the lower village, Joachim's place, spread out below, slightly hazy, slightly blue, with the church dome glinting even from that distance.

At the top village the old woman who looks after the minute taverna, a συμπεθέρα, who is connected to Vasili by marriage, served us our beer and settled in for a chat. 'I'm a foreigner here,' she declared. 'I'm from the other side of the mountain.' Her headscarf bore this statement out, for it was not tied in the local fashion. We nodded, and then she demanded to be brought up to date. A flood of questions ensued about relatives here and about my family Up There, for the concept of Down Under has always been too much to grasp. She trotted out the usual formulaic phrases on hearing of the death of my mother and quite suddenly I burst out, 'It's not fair, though, is it? My mother was quite young, and down there my mother-in-law is so old that she doesn't know where she is, what day it is, or whether she's dead or alive. It's just not fair.'

The old woman was horrified. Her head shook

slightly with indignation and she hissed at me sharply. 'Tsst. Be quiet, I tell you. What have you just said? God will cast us out if we say such things.' It was kind of her to use the plural; she, plainly, would never say such things.

Her husband emerged from the gloom of the taverna: at eighty-two, still a considerable presence. Slim and straight and handsome, like so many of the old mountain men, with a full head of hair and a most impressive white moustache, curled and twirled at the ends. He eyed me sadly. 'I *want* to die,' he announced.

'Whatever for?' I asked, while June shook her head.

'It's time,' he said gravely. 'I can't work much any more, my eyes are failing, and that's a great nuisance, and I do not want to be a burden to my children. I want to die but I can't, somehow.' He gave us both a gentle smile. There was nothing to say. We left quite soon.

That life and death are viewed differently here from Melbourne and London is obvious. The old people thought that life and death were different in America, too, but in January 1978, during our second visit to the village, Uncle Stavros's daughter, Vasili's cousin, died in Lowell, Massachusetts, during a flu epidemic. She was younger than I am now. That winter was a severe one in Greece and a very severe one in the States. Poor Uncle Stavros was totally bewildered: a place like *Ameriki*, with all that knowledge, all that science and money, and all those doctors! That she should die! It seemed impossible. He sat blinking his red-rimmed eyes, holding his walking-stick straight and striking the floor with it in a gesture of protest and incomprehension.

Every parent knows that the death of a child is the ultimate nightmare. They know about, but do not want to think about, the precariousness of life. Katie, whom Joachim knows and loves, wrote a verse about this subject once, after observing her children at play. The most memorable line went something like, 'I wish that something stronger than skin kept you in.' How every parent understands.

Artemis I feel very tired. I suppose this is natural after my long life and after all my hard work. All I want now is to sleep forever, peacefully, of course, with no dreams of strife and no δυσκολίες, no difficulties, no tossing and turning because of troubling thoughts and memories. There can't be long to wait now, but still I must be patient. Perhaps it would have been a good idea to keep walking for longer, to keep on my feet for as long as possible. Perhaps the good death, ο καλός θάνατος, would be mine now if I had done this. But one day I became so tired that I just sat down, and now I couldn't walk if I tried, or if I wanted to.

Not like my foreign *nfi*, who was always walking and wandering about, always wanting to get away. Was she looking for something? I do not know. She once asked me if I would like to go with her. Only once. I laughed at her. She needed to be taught a lesson. 'I haven't got time to waste,' I told her.

'But the mountains are so beautiful, so very beautiful,' she said quietly. Sometimes, I recall now, I used to long for her to shriek at me, to show some spirit, to show me her strength as a woman. But of course she never did: there was nothing to show. When, on that occasion, she remarked on the beauty of the mountains, I sniffed. 'If, κορίτσι μου, my girl, you had walked in them, through them, up and down them, and toiled in them ceaselessly as I have, you would not dare to talk to me about their beauty.' She said nothing, but turned away, as usual, and shortly afterwards drifted off.

She didn't stop walking in the mountains, though. The shame of it: the women used to twit me about my peculiar foreign daughter-in-law. 'Well, what can you expect, as she *is* foreign?' I said, more than once. The shame was not just connected with her walking, either. She met common people and talked to them. At length, very often. She would tell me about meeting relatives. She did not understand that there are always people, even if they are relatives, whom one does not wish to acknowledge. They know nothing and have nothing to offer. All they have is a share in our good name. This is something, it has to be said, but it is not enough.

Yet usually I did not allow any criticism whatsoever. With all her faults and failings, she was ours and had to be defended. Outsiders must not be permitted to criticise, even if they are right. The power of the family has to be guarded, shored up, at all costs. She dealt it a death-blow when she left. No wonder I am tired. And now I have no power at all, cannot help the rest of the family. Instead I am in their power, and this is a fact, a feeling, I do not like.

Yes, I feel very tired, but tonight my brain, quite unexpectedly, seems to be working well. I've even answered some of the family's questions correctly. They have been pleased with me. And Joachim is here, playing with a baby. I suppose she must be mine, this baby, a great-granddaughter, perhaps. But still nobody bears my name, Artemis. This is obviously Fate, and possibly the Evil Eye at work. Perhaps I have had too many blessings and must now be punished. It was up to the *nífi* to have a girl, but she didn't.

She, the *nífi*, was always tired. I never knew why, as she never did anything much. She never suffered, either. Not like me. She had no experience of war, of famine, of the death of children. But her life is not over yet and anything could happen. Fate and the Evil Eye might still strike her down.

Why could she not see that I was right about this

place, this world? I am right because of my long life, my knowledge, my experience in my own place, my village. Why did she expect to have my son's company? Women should not expect the company of men, should not do the things they do. What was she thinking of, wearing trousers, driving a car? She chopped wood, too. Well, that was all right. But when her father was here she mixed cement for him. She preferred mixing cement to harvesting olives. Of course she couldn't do either for very long. No strength. But she did her best for her father, tried to please him. I thought her preference very strange, but of course the foreign father didn't. She'd done it, he tried to explain, when she was a mere girl, so why should she not do it now? Why not, indeed! Some people never understand anything.

I never understood her longing for other places. She always wanted to take her boys, one or all, with her when she went, making them discontented. And she was always speaking English to them. What for? They are Greeks, my grandsons, and proud of it. They must be. That is only natural and right. She encouraged them in all the wrong things, like speaking English and attachment to animals. Animals are for work; so are wives. But then, she, the foreign wife, never accepted that. What she wanted, I never knew. Not us or our way of life, that seems certain. What *was* the matter with our place, that she was always wanting to get away?

She should have refused my son. But having

accepted him, she should have concentrated on something useful, like weaving, although that would have been far too difficult for her to learn. Eventually I could see that she was making herself ill. It had to happen: the wrong person in the wrong place, busying herself with things that are wrong. Not only wrong but useless: books and pens and paper and journeys and walking. What good are these to a wife and mother? She had no spirit, no will, no religion. She was weak in body and brain. All that weeping in the κτήματα. Yes, I knew she was becoming ill. So did my son, I am certain, although we never discussed it. Discussion of these things does not do. Separately we made the sign of the Cross and hoped and prayed that all would be well. We did our best. We have always done our best.

I r e n e   What a grey, miserable day. Such weather makes me aware of the way in which my hair resembles a Collingwood or Newcastle football jumper, and my face the network of railway tracks at Jolimont or Waterloo. But they are my campaign medals, my grey hairs and wrinkles, I've earned them. Autumn comes to everybody, after all.

So does winter. The winter of 1977/8 was much the same as that of 1975/6, except that it was much colder. It was so cold that I forgot I had feet, I wrote to my mother. I seemed to be walking around on my

ankles most of the time. The olive harvest was struggled through, somehow; Christmas came and went.
Bright days pierced the winter darkness, as they had
before. One evening we arrived at yet another ances-
tral village, deep in the mountains, just as a shepherd
was driving his flock up a slope edged with spreading
chestnut and walnut trees. The day had been fine, the
few houses were sunk in pink light, and the tinkling of
the sheep bells carried on the crisp air. Bare paddocks
and thousands of dust-clouded merinos, the scenes of
my childhood, seemed very far away.

I returned, as I often did, to Methoni, one of the
seven towns offered by Agamemnon to Achilles. I have
laughed and cried at Methoni, have felt reduced to an
infinitesimal speck by those towering castle walls
which have seen far more than I ever will. There are
long dark stains spilling over them: oil or tar, Vasili
thought. I agreed, but thought of blood, buckets of it,
as well. I visited Methoni six months before Joachim
was born. I was well, I was very happy; the wildflowers
were in full bloom. I spoke English all day because
Australian friends were visiting.

The next time I remember we were all there. So
were my parents and my great-aunt and uncle. Joachim
was two and a half, and rode crowing with joy on
Uncle Pat's broad farmer shoulders. He hung on to
Pat's ears or clung round his neck, and it was hard to
tell who wore the broader grin. I admired Joachim's

courage. Pat is over six feet tall, so Joachim must have felt very separate from the ground and certainty. But Pat is a person to trust. He is also hugely entertaining.

'This place,' he said ruminatively, 'is like that place in Rome. You know the one.' But I had never been to Rome.

'C'mon. You know. No roof. Lotta cats.'

'The Coliseum?' I hazarded.

'Yep, that's the one. What an atmosphere.'

'Sinister?' I suggested.

'Sinister? Too right. That place is as sinister as the flamin' Melbourne Cricket Ground.' I think he wondered why I became faintly hysterical.

And then I went back in 1990 and cried my eyes out because Thomas was in Australia and I was in Greece and unhappy and missing him, and because nothing would ever be the same again. I was right about that, of course. Nothing stays the same. Thomas left because he had to; I left Joachim because I had to, and the thought of the difference between being left and leaving nearly overwhelms me. I will never get over leaving Joachim, but I had to go on living, had to be a live failure rather than a dead success.

Vasili had been absent from Greece for fifteen years at the time of his return. Now we are about even. Our final departure from Melbourne was not without incident: Vasili was mistaken for a Greek currency smuggler at Tullamarine airport. Calls were made to

Russell Street police headquarters and he was subjected to the indignity of a body search. In my usual crisis state of suspended animation, I could only admire his restraint. No tantrums were forthcoming.

We stopped over at Sydney, Bali, Jakarta, Singapore, Jeddah, Athens, and finally Frankfurt, where we bought a car. Thomas and Michael disgraced us by wanting to eat at McDonald's and I plucked up enough courage to say *Briefmarken, Luftpost* in a post office, and parted with *zwei* marks for the stamps. Motivation is everything: I simply had to post my letters. I became quite bold after that and could not really understand Vasili's refusal to grapple with German. I thought he was being mulish when he said, 'I've been through this agony once. Never again.'

Now I understand completely and fall into the folds, the blanketing warmth, of English with the greatest relief. I have no desire to learn another language, or to attempt to cope with another culture. Greece and Greek have exhausted me. Joachim may not understand this because he slips and slides so easily between two cultures and fits in in both. And he is, as all my sons are, bilingual – an advantage here in Europe where one is often judged by one's ability as a linguist, by one's oral performance.

The German *autobahn* was terrifying then and it has got worse, I am told. I do not wish to know. I'm not sure what Thomas and Michael remember of it, or of

Germany, Austria and Italy. Playing football in the Black Forest? Climbing the hundreds of steps in Ulm Minster? Seeing the highest mountains of their lives in a village outside Innsbruck? Discovering Austrian and Italian food? '*Bald* spaghetti!' said Thomas in disgust, on learning that sauces had to be ordered separately, and I was instantly reminded of the Australian traveller who had not thought much of Europe. 'Why not?' someone asked. 'Tucker's off,' he replied succinctly.

Surely they must remember Venice, where Joachim has never been? He will get there one day, and doubtless it will be much the same: dirty, crumbling, and magnificent. We enjoyed ourselves in Venice. After a shaky start. Vasili reeled out of a tourist information centre muttering about Italian inflation and the millions of lire that grasping landlords were demanding from innocent, unsuspecting tourists like our good selves. As he seated himself mournfully in the car an old man wobbled up on a bicycle that looked almost as old.

'*Casa?*' he breathed hopefully.

'*Casa*,' replied Vasili, also hopefully.

'*Bella casa!*' said the ancient.

And off we set. He guided us, sketching hand signals and weaving all over the road, to what was indeed a *bella casa*. Thomas and Michael charmed the signor and the signora, and Vasili, despite his moans about German, was very happy to practise his hundred words of Italian. As for myself, I was very happy to see a spotless bedroom: signora had embroidered *buona notte* on each pillowslip, and that seemed to be a sort of guarantee.

In the morning signora beamed, handed us a map, and pointed us in the direction of the Grand Canal. It was fearfully hot, I recall, and tempers, not just ours, were frayed. A middle-aged gentleman shepherded his family on to the *vaporetto*, which was very crowded, and then had the misfortune to be left behind: the attendant fastened the chain and that was that. The rage that ensued was operatic: loud and prolonged, the main theme of which, I gathered, was that the *vaporetto* attendant was an *analfabeta porco*. This, I thought, in school-teacherly fashion, was an interesting example of redundancy, for surely all pigs are illiterate?

Next day signor and signora were in despair at the thought of us driving to Brindisi, and muttered darkly about the population south of, yes, well, Venice. Ancona? we suggested, and they pulled long faces and said well, yes, we might, just might, manage to be safe there, but the *bambini* . . . signora held up her hands. So long a journey. So far. Tell her the *bambini* are tough, I told Vasili. And they were.

And so, later, was Joachim, trailing round Crete in a three-generation travelling party at the age of five, eating φασολάκια, green beans, until they came out of his ears, and being very patient at Knossos, Phaistos, and in countless museums. There were lighter moments, like the one in which he fairly hopped with glee when my father drank too much retsina.

'You've disgraced us all,' my mother intoned, her tee-total soul quite revolted at the sight of her husband of forty-five years swaying on the footpath in Heraklion.

'I'm not drunk,' he announced.

'Walk that line,' I commanded, and would not have been able to do it myself.

'Blame that waiter from Sydney,' he mumbled as we steered him back to the hotel.

But I digress. The four of us got to Ancona safely. Vasili and the Italian sailors screamed and swore at each other with great vivacity and verve, but we boarded the appropriately named *Kangaroo* eventually, and sailed across the dark-blue Adriatic. Greece lay in wait. And so, thank God, did Joachim.

While Joachim and I were both waiting, some semblance of routine was established, even though Vasili and I both felt rather lost and adrift. The dizzying speed with which modern modes of transport dump people on the opposite side of the world has that effect. But it, our stay in Greece, still seemed only a holiday, and we divided our time between the beach and the piece of land on the other side of the Athens road, where Vasili's brother Thothoro had established an enormous vegetable garden. I continued to report our doings.

July 1980
The beach

Kindly note the address above and please
excuse smears of suntan cream, grains of sand,
etc. The weather is absolutely perfect here,
with cloudless skies and high temperatures
and cool nights.

Well, so far, so good, though even Vasili
admits to feeling lost. I must say I feel rather
strange myself. Melbourne seems very far
away.

The boys were impressed recently by the
sight of a little tortoise, some cicadas, several
frogs, and a hedgehog, which their aunt
caught and wrapped up in a piece of plastic.

Much later, Joachim had a pet hedgehog called
Hercules which was kept in a large cage until he
became neurotic, pacing – well, waddling – up and
down and had to be set free. I wonder if Joachim
remembers. Hercules was a sweet creature with a snuf-
fling snout and a delicate pink mouth. But one evening
cousin Leo gave him a dead bird and in the morning
there was not a trace of the corpse left. Not a trace.

In 1980 various problems began to present themselves and refused to go away. The battle with the
Greek bureaucracy, which to this day seems to want to
strangle itself and a patient public in reams of red tape,

was one; the struggle to get Thomas and Michael to do their English correspondence lessons was another. At the end of a month I was already moaning to my long-suffering mother.

August 1980

I might as well be on a desert island here as far as news goes. I have managed to get hold of the *Times* twice, but for all I know the third world war could be raging. Vasili says it's better not knowing about current affairs, but I can't agree.

We are settling into the routine here. Twice a week we go to the vegetable garden and I help by controlling the little irrigation channels with my hoe. The other day I helped Thothoro tie up frames for the beans, and lug home a bundle of orange-tree branches for the goat. Thothoro thinks this incursion into rural activity very funny and says I should have my photograph taken while at work.

Then there was Yiayia, who flatly refused to believe that the walls of Ancient Ithome were built by mortal man. They erupted like mountains from the earth, she maintained. Of course there is quite some excuse for this belief; that in itself was not a problem. Rather it was Yiayia's dogmatism which upset me. I never did get used to it. I hope Joachim will understand this. And that was not all.

> I feel rather like a fifth wheel. Vasili, running true to form, goes out every night to the *kafeneion*. I'm also feeling rather like the dependent female, as Vasili has been very reluctant to let me drive the car – because of the narrow streets, he says. I've insisted, and have managed three successful trips so far. I'm too used to doing my own thing, and it's just not that simple here . . . I've got to assert myself. It's all quite an ordeal, particularly being stared at in the street. I think Greek men must have the most penetrating stares in the world.

Things became worse quite soon, as Thomas and Michael started school, as I became lonelier and felt more isolated. Juliet was there in the village, but some time passed before I met her. The summer had been very busy, and then, at first, I found her difficult to know. This was my fault in a way, because I am shy and easily daunted by other people, am often quite misanthropic. Juliet's tranquillity made me feel uncomfortable. She seemed to have worked everything out, was not impatient, was not rebellious. Her Greek was excellent and her child was well behaved and well adjusted. I was jealous of her happiness. In time, I came to know her and to understand that, like most people, she had earned it. Now we are firm friends, even though, or perhaps because, we are so different. She has always been good to me; she is a good person.

Way back then it was also difficult to work: reading and writing were for school-children, not for grown-up females who were supposed to excel as housewives and hostesses and nothing much else. I did not rate very high on this scale. But then, as now, I continued to be entertained and mystified by turns. At the *kafeneion* I saw an old man wearing two sets of glasses, one for the close reading of his newspaper and one for viewing the life of the street. Ten years later Vasili started doing exactly the same thing, so that he could read a newspaper and watch television more or less simultaneously. Old women wore their headscarves even while splashing in the waves of Messinian Bay.

Near the time for the exhumation of Yiayia's priesthusband's body, I was with her when she walked calmly into a shop in Kalamata, purchased a blue charnel-house box with a red cross outlined on it, and ordered her husband's initials to be painted on it while she waited. There seemed little to say.

Joachim will not remember Yiayia weaving. Neither do I, actually, but she told me about all that hard work and gave me a few things she had made. I had never imagined a handwoven petticoat, of all garments, but I have one – unworn, of course. The frame of her loom still stands on the πατοματάκι, that mezzanine floor where the essential work of the house used to be done. It was Amy of the fine, perceptive mind who pointed out the metaphor of cloth for the situation I soon found myself in.

The vocabulary of weaving is odd in English. I'm sure Joachim will think the Old English words 'warp' and 'weft' quite strange. I'll have to point out that the warp is the long thread, and the weft the short ones which cross them. To Amy, the warp was our home country, and the weft the countries we seek. We weave a pattern of past and present, of horizontal and vertical affections. Perhaps love is the shuttle? Love and hope. My particular shuttle kept flying back and forth for a very long time, but now it has stuck fast and I can neither rethread the loom nor cut the long bolt of material free. Perhaps I had too many hopes, too much determination, placed too much faith in the efficacy of work and good intentions. It is hard to know, and how important is this knowledge now, anyway?

J u l i e t   I've had an exhausting evening at school. Some of these classes are not going well and I can't seem to do much about them. Sometimes I don't feel I have any control over this endless routine, and that's one of the things teachers dread most – loss of control. Loss of power. But control and power, surely, are proved every day to be an illusion, and not just to teachers.

It's interesting, the way in which we construct our routines, build our illusions, in an effort to keep functioning. Who was it who wrote that life consists simply of waiting for something awful to happen and trying not to think about it? Irene must have quoted that to me. We used to be, Irene and I, pretty good at practising the noble art of distraction.

She used to be an optimist, too, but isn't any more. I've the routine of teaching. Hers was based on endless activity of an intellectual type: French lessons, Greek lessons, reading of all sorts, writing of all sorts. Teaching and housework fitted in somehow. She used to do everything quickly, but near the end she slowed almost to a stop and did nothing except the household tasks, and those she did automatically. Near the end she couldn't even read.

Anybody wanting to empty that house will have to start with a dozen drayloads of books. The shelving is not adequate: books creep up walls in neat piles, and stacks of yellowing newspapers still sit in every corner. There were bags and boxes of letters. Even now, she tells me, she is never without her plastic bag of letters to be answered. Aristides and Petros at the post office dreaded the days they had no letters for her; it was plain to them, although they couldn't understand it, really, that she was lost without her letters. Once, they said, they feared for her sanity during a postal strike. It's only a strike, Aristides told her, it will end. But when? she asked, stricken, and he couldn't bear to meet her eyes. And now she writes to Joachim nearly every day. I never knew there were so many different postcards in London.

It seems obvious, now, that this small world wasn't enough for her. It's been said often that women tend to strike bargains they don't understand. Well, men do, too, I suppose, although the men I know are, and have been, very clear-eyed, not to mention self-interested, in what they take on. For Irene, marriage meant a contraction of her world in a way she couldn't immediately foresee, and didn't guess at at the time. Difference, at least to the inexperienced, so often seems enticing, masquerades as an expansion of the most tempting kind. When the dif-ference reveals itself, after a time, to be a shrinking, a steady contraction, it becomes the heaviest of burdens.

I think Irene once believed that people are much the same the world over, and she learned the hard way that this simply isn't true. Place, background, religion, class: they all count. Quite suddenly she found herself in a country where there are always set rules. It's easy to see how these same rules attracted her initially, for it's part of her nature, I've discovered, to long for certainty, secu-rity, permanence, and she's always had very clear rules for her own life. Do your best, be honest, work hard, try hard, persist, be brave, don't hurt other people. Ironic, now, to think of them. All societies have rules, obviously; most individuals have them. But hers, whatever else can be said of them, weren't lived from a sense of habit.

Here I sit, concentrating on Irene because that, at the moment, seems the simplest thing to do. It is easier to dwell on her problems, particularly now that she is so far away, than on my own. Irene's a limpet by nature: she clings to the people and places she likes and finds it impossible to let go of the people who are still in the places she's had to leave. That's why she was obsessed with the post office. What she'd left was a middle-class milieu, a degree of urbanity and bookishness which she wasn't ever going to find here. She tried very hard, at one stage, to shift the family to Athens. I remember that effort well: it failed. There were a great many efforts which produced no result; that's the way things are here.

As the years passed it became obvious that she needed something to replace what she'd lost, and so the search, the expansion, started. At the very least she needed variety, flexibility, curiosity, an open way of looking at things. She is, after all, of pioneer stock. Pioneers, it seems to me, make things up as they go along, in response to particular situations. That's the approach she took here in the village at first, never dreaming that here, as there are set situations, so there are set responses to them. Eventually she applied herself with great tenacity to expanding her own world. This expansion was necessary for her sons, too, she believed, and so she took them away whenever she could, and when she couldn't, ensured that there was a steady stream of foreign visitors to the house.

Perhaps this tenacity, these efforts, were not a good idea. Perhaps her sons feel badly done by, feel that they don't quite fit. It's hard to know. What I do know something about is the difficulty of living in two worlds. Irene spent all her money on travel, and is obviously still doing so. I spent mine on my house. It might've been better if she'd done the same. But then, I, Juliet, and she, Irene, are very different.

I can't write any more tonight. I wish I could say, with equal certainty, that I won't *think* any more tonight.

Tomorrow, Irene remembers suddenly, is Thomas's birthday. Oceans divide them: she posted his present months ago, for he is still in Melbourne, where he was born. She has always considered that Thomas has done well for himself: not only was he born on a Sunday, but that particular Sunday was the Feast Day of the Holy Wisdom, the day of wisdom, faith, hope and love. Remembering the efforts her parents made the year before, Irene thinks this birthday will not be such a happy one. They decorated the house down to the last inch and then went away for the weekend. And now Thomas's grandmother has gone away again, but not just for the weekend.

Melbourne used to be called marvellous Melbourne. Irene also thinks of it as magnetic Melbourne, because it keeps drawing her back. It is motherly as well, she considers, because she grew up there and associates it with deep memories of being cared for, cherished and nurtured in a secure environment. She knows it was not really like this, knows she is viewing it through the rose-coloured spectacles on issue to every expatriate, knows she is forgetting the numbers who fled old narrownesses, provincialism and prejudices. She realises she has chosen to ignore the ugly things, the rejections, the hurts, the mean passage of time. She realises that Melbourne and she have both changed and will keep on changing.

Irene considers it quite likely that Thomas has his own pair of rose-coloured glasses focused on Greece. His father's spectacles are photochromatic and become still pinker with the passing of time. Greece never lost its rosy glow for him. Irene wonders whether the word to describe Vasili's spectacles should be chronophotochromatic. She also considers that, as she feels about Melbourne, so her boys will feel about the village.

Irene's vivid memories of Melbourne are of the city

as it was, but now her memories of her old self are blurred, definitely wavy around the edges.

I r e n e   Melbourne in spring. It is Royal Show time there, and Grand Final time.

The pink-and-white and flame-red japonicas will be in full bloom, globes of passionfruit will be purpling slowly, the prunus trees will be a riot of blossom, and in the 'English' suburbs like Camberwell and Hawthorn and Kew, gardeners will be feeling that life has meaning again. Old women will be tottering along, periodically leaning over fences to say things like 'What glorious daffs. *And* the freesias. Those dahlias are coming on nicely. Strange how Iceland poppies have gone out of fashion, don't you think?' Early tourists will note the floral clock in St Kilda Road, stroll in the Domain and the Royal Botanic Gardens, and realise why Victoria is called the garden state.

I don't think young people notice the turn of the seasons much, beyond feeling thankful that the warmer weather and holidays are on the way, or mournful and gloomy because both are over. Thomas is far more interested in clothes, sport and enjoying himself. When Michael was visiting in Melbourne last month, the pair of them rang me up on my birthday.

'Are you having a good time?' I asked.

'Yeah,' said Thomas, who thinks I am very shock-able. 'Yeah. Drinking, gambling and womanising.'

'Not all at once, I hope,' I replied, determined not to react. He'll be back in Greece soon, and I'm starting to wonder already about his warp and weft, about his horizontal and vertical affections for Australia and Greece.

It has been said that London defies the imagination and breaks the heart. The former, yes, the latter no, at least not so far. People are the heart-breakers, although, on reflection, perhaps it is the interaction of people and places which is so important, which does the damage. Places change people, too, I think. I am certainly not the person I was in Australia.

I had not been in the village very long before my wayward, unruly locks needed cutting. We, as a family, have a great talent for growing hair. Yiayia showed me the hairdresser's shop and told me to get on with it. So I did. The old building is one of the village originals, most of which are disappearing fast. The door is right on the street. I turned the ancient knob and entered, squinting in the gloom, for the place was lit by only two little skylights. The dusty bare boards were relieved only by a minute square of hand-woven rug in the doorway and a little table on which a few droop-ing fern fronds in a vase tried to make a brave show of it. The dingy walls were covered with photos of mod-els showing the latest outlandish hairstyles.

The hairdresser was a very pretty girl, a 'sweet young thing blatantly bottle-blonde', as I wrote to my mother. She greeted me pleasantly, asked me what I wanted, and then proceeded to slop what looked like green dish-washing liquid all over my head. Rinse over, she produced an antique pair of scissors which clashed ominously with each unconfident snip. Then it was the turn of the *pistolaki*, the 'little pistol' hairdryer, with which she burnt my scalp with great dedication for ten minutes. Finally, my poor hair, rapidly turning white I felt sure, as a result of this treatment, was teased and sprayed. I paid a minuscule sum and tottered out, feeling that I needed the rest of the day in which to recover.

Now when I am in the village I go to another hairdresser. After all these years I still brace myself, for in the space of a day London disappears and I take a plunge back into a world of intense religiosity, superstition and black magic, where the talk is of spells, curses, miracles, witches and weeping icons. Panayota snips and develops her various conspiracy theories, murmuring matter-of-factly about Jews and Masons. I must tell Joachim that discretion is the better part of valour: I have certainly never told Panayota that both my grandfathers were Masons, although I believe Michael once electrified a religious studies lesson by imparting this piece of information. The teacher cried, «Παναγία» – 'Our Lady' – fervently and crossed herself.

I am jealous of their certainties, just as I am jealous of the fact that some of the women here are so old while my mother did not have the chance to be. Robed in black, they creep slowly along the streets and lanes, looking worn, looking desiccated. They have had very hard lives, but now it seems to me that their lack of choice has worked to conserve their energy.

When I think of the old women and their certainties, I also think of Juliet and her religious convictions, that enviable faith. She has an absolute reliance on God which I would give anything to possess. I am not an atheist, but my narrow religious upbringing has made me rather resentful of God; my grandmothers insisted that He knew everything. If He knew about every sparrow that fell, He was also the One from whom no secrets were hid. The idea made me fearful and cross; later I concluded that God was not a democrat at all, otherwise He would value liberty and privacy more.

God keeps Juliet going. I suppose this thought borders on blasphemy, but my mother used to keep me going: the support of the weekly letter, full of good sense, the occasional phone call, the knowledge that she was in her place, getting on with things on the other side of the world. She expended her energy recklessly, though, with all her doubts and worry, with her unselfishness and multiple outgoings. 'Your mother has gone to Charos,' said old Maria, our neighbour, her ancient eyes staring into mine. «Τι να κάνουμε; What can we do? Ζωή σε σας. Life to you.'

Now my mother is gone and I am gone from Joachim, and my world, relentlessly contracting in spite of geographical appearances to the contrary, turns very slowly in these absences. There is another absence, too, which it is futile to mention.

I am slowly getting through the pile of old letters. Some of them are very personal, and I have no intention of telling Joachim many of the things which I wrote to his grandparents all those years ago. It would not do at all, would only upset him. But the pattern which had begun in Melbourne kept on weaving itself, or being woven, I am not sure which, kept working itself out, I know now, with the inexorability of a Greek tragedy.

Last November, here in London, I went to see a production of Euripides' *Medea*, and sat helpless and racked with regret of the most painful sort as Medea, the foreign wife, raged at Jason, that master of self-justification. Years ago Vasili and I went to Epidaurus to see *The Oresteian Trilogy*. The late Melina Mercouri played Clytemnestra. Interesting, the contrasts in Greek tragedy: the apparent impotence and yet strange, sheer power of the women, who act decisively when driven and desperate. Primitive in a way many men could not understand then and cannot understand now. I remember Mercouri, but not the name of the actor who played Agamemnon. I remember only the moment of his doom, sealed as he stepped onto the purple carpet.

I have been back to Epidaurus twice since, to see *Prometheus Bound* and *Hecuba*. Joachim was not with me to see the wedge-shaped set that Prometheus was chained to, to see him slide swiftly away into blackness at the end of the play, to see the chorus dancing sinuously, concealed in light-blue masks, swathed in lycra costumes and wraps. He was, however, with me at the performance of *Hecuba*, and fell asleep, his head on my lap, while the chorus circled and lamented, while worlds met and collided: cameras flashed incessantly and an aeroplane droned overhead as the ancient and not-so-ancient passions were being re-enacted.

I wrote home again soon after that first visit to Epidaurus.

August 1980

We have been offered part-time jobs which
we will probably accept. Vasili is desperate to
stay. I don't know. We'll see. I'm dreading
sending Thomas and Michael to school here.
Don't worry. I'll survive. I always do.

The point was, though, that I very nearly didn't. Twelve summers later I had reached the point where the war of attrition, the corrosive effect of difference

116

and indifference and what I saw as a hundred betrayals of all sorts, the slow accumulation of pain and disappointment, the sense of loss of self, all threatened to engulf me. I had had to function on the edge of a world which did not know me and did not want to. For all these reasons, and for some others that I cannot bear to think about, I could not keep the machinery working, not even – and I hate myself for this, and will do so as long as I live – for Joachim's sake.

Depression is not sensible, not profitable, but comes – often – because of a sense of wasted effort, because of disillusionment. I was as childlike as Joachim is for a long, long time after my thirteenth birthday, for I believed that if I kept on trying, kept on working hard, kept on being *good*, everything would be all right. Things, however, kept going wrong, and I was finally forced to acknowledge that they would continue to do so, and to accept the fact that some of my wounds, along with my divided heart, were never going to heal.

It has been said that the heart is a little thing and one can coerce it. I tried to coerce mine but could not do so, and then it, the wilful, wayward creature, made, it seems to me, a unilateral decision to go its own way. Head, will, reason, conscience had no effect at all, except to ensure a long period of grief and conflict.

I seem to have become part of the civilisation of luggage as I search for home and succeed only in approximating it. My restless junketings: Australia, England, Greece. And now home and childhood too have gone forever, because my mother is dead. Now the whole world is a foreign land.

But it is still autumn in the village, the morning glories will be unrolling everywhere, and from the upstairs window the eight olive trees will still be seen standing behind Kyria Konstantina's house. The pomegranate and the almond trees are there, and it will not be long before plumes of smoke will start to brush the morning and evening light.

Soon, and he will moan about this, Joachim will have to start the business of fetching and carrying from the woodheap to the stove. Thomas and Michael, when they were little, were supposed to take bundles of sticks to school. Yiayia, resenting the inroads on her neatly stacked pile of wood, soon baulked at this. 'Tell the teachers you're foreign', she urged them, 'and that this is not a custom where you come from.'

Nice try, Yiayia, they said, or words to that effect, and kept obeying their teachers. Now Yiayia does not know who her grandsons are, and fires no longer burn on the kitchen hearth because of the danger of rolling logs. It is no longer possible to cut a lump of sausage from the strings hanging inside the chimney. Those days are gone.

I am living new days, and when Joachim comes to visit I'll take him to Parliament Hill, where there is nearly always somebody, at least, flying a kite. Joachim does not study English history, but I'll tell him that legend has it that in 1605 the Roman Catholic conspirators, having put barrels of gunpowder in the cellars of the Houses of Parliament, optimistically sat up on Parliament Hill and waited for the Houses to blow up. The Gunpowder Plot was discovered and they were arrested instead.

The kites, like their flyers, come in all shapes and sizes. I like to think they can tell their own stories of what they see of the mighty heart of London, tell tales of close encounters way up there above the earth. Trust *you*, Mum, to think of things like that, I hear Joachim saying. When he comes we'll go to a kite shop I've been told about, and we'll buy something economical and easy, and he can teach me how to fly it. How long ago it seems since I discovered that the Greek for kite is 'paper eagle'. I still like that.

Thomas and Michael could have flown kites from near the Temple of Apollo Epikourios at Bassae, which Joachim has also seen. Now it has been spoiled, with the best of motives, has had a stiff white tent placed over it in order to protect it. The tent is held in place by gigantic plaited-steel cables; Vasili is much admiring of the engineering.

The first time the older boys and I visited this temple I had no idea it was a thousand metres above sea level and so remote from everything else. June was with us and we had not realised, either of us, when studying the map that most of the road had yet to be made. It took us two hours to travel forty kilometres; the sweat that poured out of me was as much from anxiety and downright fear as from the heat. The track was rutted and narrow. June, who does not drive, developed the annoying habit of saying, 'Gosh. Sheer drop on this side.'

We crawled up and up through bare mountains which swept away as far as the eye could see. Both my eyes were firmly fixed on the miserable roadway ahead; at one stage, to my horror, I could see another car approaching. By great good luck both vehicles met on a stretch a little wider than the rest. We stopped and a weary Frenchman asked, '*Combien de kilomètres à Tolon?*' – Tolon being the place we had left behind. '*Trente,*' I replied succinctly. '*Mon Dieu,*' he said, rather desperately, and crossed himself. I felt sorry for him, but rather sorrier for myself, not having a clear idea of how much further we ourselves had to go.

But every trial comes to an end, as I hope Joachim will learn. Like a miracle a great grey structure reared from its barren setting. June cried, 'The temple!' but I, the philistine, gasped with relief and said, 'Thank God. An asphalt road.'

There is still nothing there except this mighty edifice brooding over vast landscape, this monument to Apollo the healer, built in thanks by people who had escaped the ravages of plague. Joachim was older when he saw it than his brothers had been at the time of their visit, and more impressed, although I think he liked Andritsaina better. He's Greek, after all, and loves company. But at least he looked at the temple and admired it.

In Andritsaina he had his photo taken near the eighteenth-century drinking fountain and I noticed then, for the first time, how long his legs were growing. The old men still puff along the winding, sloping streets, leaning heavily on their walking-sticks, or sit at *kafeneion* tables drinking coffee and fingering their worry beads and drooping moustaches in turn, waiting for somebody to talk to.

Every so often, or more frequently, worlds collide: I have had this thought before. I walked, gaping, into the British Museum on my very first visit and had not got very far at all when I was stopped in my tracks by a photograph of this very temple of Apollo. I suppose I knew, but had forgotten, that the frieze from the temple is in the museum. So upstairs I went and gaped further. There is no point in trying to describe it. It is something Joachim can see for himself when he comes, if he wants to.

In 1980 I recovered more quickly from anxiety, suspense and flirtations with danger than I do now, and two days after the excursion to Bassae I set off into the mountains again, this time on foot and with Vasili and his cousin. The only person we met on the way was a boy of about thirteen. He was jogging along on a donkey, far from anyone and anywhere, and reading a Western as he rode. I liked the idea of his solitude, his self-containedness, and the familiarity yet strangeness of his reading matter.

At our destination, a place consisting of a well and a church and not much more, we met the parents of a distant cousin of Vasili's. Theo and his wife had been living in Prahran, Melbourne, increasingly homesick for Greece, and decided to return home to their village. They sold or shipped everything and set off. And then, and then . . . they took one look at the village of their fondest memories and dreams and hated it, and were back in Melbourne while their washing-machine was still on the high seas. A familiar story, as was the parents' disappointment.

Nobody expected us to stay in Greece. They all thought we wouldn't, couldn't possibly, do it, but we did. Even then, though, I was preoccupied with stories of people who had been forced into exile.

In 1980 Irene sent her parents a newspaper cutting about the thirty-six islanders who had in 1930 been made to leave St Kilda, a dotlike place in the Atlantic, off the west coast of Scotland. They were evacuated to the mainland because they were in danger of starving, having been permitted to take their wild sheep with them. At the very peak of development the settlement had consisted of only one street and sixteen stone houses. For nine months of the year St Kilda was cut off from the rest of the world by bad weather. There was no radio communication, and urgent messages were 'posted' in a hollowed-out boat-shaped piece of driftwood attached to a sheep's bladder and sent off on the tide in a westerly wind. This is a degree of isolation that Irene, who has endured isolation enough, can only marvel at. A photograph of some island women accompanied the cutting. Dour faces. Predictable: all that bare rock, hard work and bitter cold. Irene would dearly like to know whether mainland Scotland was to them a place of unbelievable comfort, even luxury, or merely an approximation of home.

She wonders, occasionally, whether it might not be wise to give up the concept of home completely and go all out for fantasy. Recently, almost by accident, she found herself in the English Brighton, which gave her an unexpected insight into the vision the Melburnian founding fathers had tried to realise when they built their own Brighton: the promenade, the piers, the bathing boxes, the great sweep of buildings along the water.

The Royal Pavilion, she will tell Joachim, was built

by the prince who became George IV of England. Two hundred years later, Irene speculates that he might have made a reasonable Minister for the Arts, with his long-range ambitions and magnificent fantasies. The Pavilion, that dream by the sea, could never have been a home, thinks Irene. It is rather a world, with its roof-line a mixture of onion domes, Oriental inverted teardrops and ridged columns; its ceilings resembling skies, suns or huge tents; its extravagance and opulence; its gilded dragons and twining serpents. She will tell Joachim of the 36-course meals and the twelve cooks. She has no idea whether the prince was warm or comfortable, but it is obvious to her that the whole place must have needed a fearful amount of dusting. Not that there is much dust in England, she considers: it's not like the Peloponnese or the Wimmera at all.

I r e n e By October 1980 we had started our working lives, Vasili and I dividing our time between town and village. Thomas and Michael had begun attending the village school and I remember that Michael told his class the village was better than Australia because there were no robbers about. I tried to send people at home slices of Peloponnesian life and they sent me slices of theirs, cuttings as well as letters.

Many thanks for keeping the news up to the troops, who find it hard to keep in touch. I'm going to develop into an eccentric, though, sitting here chuckling over newspaper clippings from the Antipodes.

As for school, I'd forgotten just how irritating male adolescents can be. And their names! There are Spiros and Kostases galore, several by the name of Haralambos, and one Chrysovalantos, which means, I'm told, golden purse. Just imagine bearing that burden.

At the moment I am queen of this domain, Yiayia having gone to Athens. This is the second day and all livestock are well. Touch wood. The hens have laid four eggs. (Now that *is* satisfying, finding fresh eggs!) But I find hens repulsive when they are moulting; so far I have managed to avoid donkey kicks and bites. Vasili and I also have had to add sugar to the grape juice, which we hope is now busily fermenting in the big barrel downstairs.

Thomas had to be taken to the local dentist, who is a kind enough man, but tough. No mucking about, no injections, just straight into drilling. Men don't cry, he announced, in between whimpers and choking noises.

We had a quick trip to Athens ourselves, during which we did battle with the bureaucracy and realised a few modest hopes, like having hot, soaking baths – the first in four months.

Back home, as it was to him, Vasili had certain ambitions.

November 1980
Vasili is now keen to acquire another goat and
to establish a rabbit-run. I must say I prefer
my rabbit stew as depersonalised as possible,
but I suppose I should overcome such scruples.
It will be interesting to see who does the
killing should this project ever come to pass.

It never did.

Then the olive harvest was upon us. I did my share of the work and felt that my tree-climbing youth had not been wasted. I was still young enough to scramble up trees, even though my sons find this hard to believe now. In between beating olive branches I sent out more than fifty pieces of Christmas mail. As with every season in Greece, Christmas had its ups and downs.

December 1980
Christmas dinner was transported live on the
bus from Kalamata: numerous birds stowed in

the luggage compartment underneath. Fortunately. Just imagine what would have happened to all the little black headscarves had the feathered friends been arranged in rows along the luggage racks.

I've discovered that I do not want to touch turkeys. This noble bird's legs were tied together and its wings were clipped. Yiayia asked me to shift it out of the rain. Do you know how big turkeys' beaks are? I tried one lunge at his legs and found them to be disagreeably warm and scaly to the touch. I was so revolted, not to mention timorous, that I got Yiayia to move him. The condemned creature was allowed to strut in coloured majesty around the yard for a few hours before nephew Leo arrived with a knife in his hand and a murderous glint in his eye. Every part of the corpse was used – the innards as *mageritsa* – I did not get much of a thrill out of seeing two halves of turkey's stomach hanging over the kitchen tap. There is some remedy in which this is used, apparently; whether it's applied internally or externally, I don't know.

The village was struck by a violent hailstorm. It was so bad that a shower of hailstones fell continuously through the roof for a quarter of an hour. I had them in my hair!

Christmas was a grey, bitter day, but I coped reasonably well with my thoughts of home.

Nothing seemed to be easy, it's true, but I coped better in the beginning. I wonder now, looking back, what the turning point was, when the novelty wore off and the attrition set in. My letters seemed to be nothing so much as bulletins from the battlefield. Back then I described the situation as being a cross between a harem, purdah and a convent.

February 1981

I have bought a bike and have been riding about three kilometres a day, invariably meeting Papastathi on his donkey. We both pretend not to see each other. Once he asked Yiayia how her daughter-in-law the African was getting on . . .

I have been feeling very low lately.

I just have to keep hanging on.

I miss you horribly.

There has been pressure from various people to move to Kalamata, but I did not move this huge distance away in order to live in a different kind of suburbia.

I've had Michael to the doctor twice. The doctor's surgery is horrifying, like a medical desert. He listened to Michael's chest, which was okay, but that was all. I matter-of-factly requested an ear examination. Sorry, the doctor said, I haven't got the appropriate instrument. My jaw hung slack. So the village is too poor to buy these things, but doesn't he have a little black bag of his own, for Heaven's sake? I felt like saying it would be a good idea for him to go without a pair of Italian shoes once in a while and buy a few things . . . I devoutly hope none of us gets really sick.

I will be glad when I have my own house where I can shut myself up and ignore the mounting dust. People here think it is immoral for a woman, especially a wife and mother, to read or write during the day. If you're not doing something with immediate results, and preferably something ostentatiously active, then you're not achieving anything.

All is gaiety at the moment as it is carnival time. I went to school last Friday to find the whole place virtually knee-deep in confetti. I left with a goodly proportion of it in my hair and received a mouthful of it on leaving. I was not amused.

I should have been amused. I should have been more relaxed, for I see now how important it is to hang on to your child's mind for as long as you can. If you can do this, you continue to see things which adults cannot see, having lost the art of looking. Thomas, I remember, had the art of listening as well. When he was a tiny boy, my mother taught him to sing 'Lavender Blue'. He loved it and used to sing it in the car, but whenever we drove up to a house he knew to be Greek he would immediately start translating the words. I seem to remember the untranslatable 'dilly dilly' being pronounced with a Greek accent. He hardly had to draw breath in order to change languages and I was fascinated by the way in which he fitted the new words to the tune.

Michael was of a more philosophical bent. He was only four when, helping me dry dishes one night, he asked with a deeply earnest air of inquiry, 'Why did God make the world and us?' Never a quick thinker, I hadn't found a reply before he did and I almost broke a plate. 'I suppose He did it because He was lonely.'

I must tell Joachim that here in London, on a wall inside St Sophia's Cathedral in Moscow Road, there is a memorial tablet to two Greek soldiers who fell for England and for Liberty, during the First World War. Where were their mothers? I wondered. In Greece or England?

On my first Candlemas here I went to St Sophia's and wept, thinking of Joachim and the procession in Kalamata. And wept again at Christmastime when, after feeling quite reasonable one minute, I fell into a crumpled heap on entering the Gates of Mystery/Art of Holy Russia exhibition at the Victoria and Albert Museum. It was the first whiff of incense that set me off, and all those memories – the recollection of being in Constantinople. And the sight of the icon of the Mother of God of Tenderness in which the child has His cheek laid against His Mother's. I mopped my eyes for at least half an hour. My sons would not have been pleased. Thank God the lights were low.

I learned a lot, however. I like the process of learning. I learned that Vladimir of Kiev's ambassadors to the city were dazzled during that visit in the tenth century. 'We did not know,' they reported, 'if we were in Heaven or on earth; we only know that God dwells there among men, for we cannot forget that beauty.' I learned that the Panagia's robe and belt protected God-guarded Constantinople for centuries and that the Russian emperor always wore robes of red, the colour of the resurrected Christ, at Easter. And something else I learned: the difficulty, the impossibility, of dismantling a life. Orthodoxy has surrounded me for nearly thirty years.

A r t e m i s   Tonight there is a fire on the hearth, for the October evenings are becoming cooler. The family only lights a fire these days when there are visitors. In the past I was the one who controlled the fire, but now they all think it is not safe for me to have a fire burning while I am alone. Not that I am ever alone for very long. The people from my past are here in the room with me: my mother and father, my brothers and sisters, my husband. But my first family is mentioned very seldom, and my children say they are all dead, these people. That is true, but they are not dead to me. They come and they go. Sometimes they sit beside me and talk to me. And I? I always talk to them, at least in my head. My head, in fact, is rarely a quiet place. Time passes more easily when they are here. They, or their spirits. It hardly matters.

The fire is flickering. I hear the occasional rush of gas; I see the leaping blue flame. The visitors, people I do not know, have come to see my children and now have gone. They bent over me, one by one, and shook my hand. I greeted them from force of habit and custom, and was glad to see my children grilling sausage and making toast and oil, bringing out the feta cheese, being hospitable. Glad, but not surprised. I have, after all, always done my best. I have trained my children well in the sacred tradition of φιλοξένια, of hospitality.

I thought perhaps that the foreign *nifi* was among the visitors. But no, she was not here. I would have recognised her. She, too, used to have visitors, quite a lot of them. Women: tall, good-looking, strong women from Australia. Families with children not like us, with fair hair and φακίδες, freckles. Some of these people were total strangers, even to her; some of them did not even speak Greek. My son put up with them all, trying to make and keep his wife happy.

Some people are not made for happiness. This is what I believe. I, for one, never expected to be happy, never even thought about the business of happiness very much until lately. I thought about safety, about protecting seven little children from every form of evil: war, poverty, hunger. I didn't think about getting up at three in the morning to bake bread; I didn't think about the endless hours spent in the olive groves, and at the loom, for there was never any point in thinking. Such things must be done. That is the way life is. So I worked and watched my children grow. And then they left me. That is natural and right. Well, I suppose it is, but I never liked the idea. Most of the children did not go very far. No, I do not ask myself whether I have been happy.

I do not cry. Tears are a sign of weakness. Weakness is a luxury at best, a sin at worst, and I have never been able to afford either, luxury being bad for the body and sin bad for the soul. But η Παναγία, our All-Holy Mother, knows that I wept in the olive groves when my eldest son left on such a long journey. Perhaps I could be forgiven.

And then, much later, a merciful God brought my son, my beautiful one, back. I lit a very large candle in church that week, I remember. The flame burned steadily for a long while, much as the flames of the fire are burning tonight. My gratitude is with me still, for so many of the villagers left and never returned. Thothoro, Panayioti, and the rest: I forget their names, as I forget so much now.

And now, as I sit here, I am forgetting again, forgetting even my last thought, which has just slipped away. Two or three people are still here: my daughter, my son, Joachim. As long as the fire is alight they will stay. I stare into the flames and try to concentrate. *Nai*, yes, he came back, that is it, that is what I was thinking about. Now I remember that everything seemed to go well at first. They, the little family, *my* little family lived with me for quite some time.

Everything she wanted she got, my foreign *nfi*. She liked going out, so they went out. She liked going out too much. But she learned to dance, and she danced well. I will say that for her. I don't suppose she dances now. Or, if she does, she does not dance the *kalamatianó*. She has left all that behind. And her son, of course. My little Ιωακείμ. I wonder if she has found new mountains to climb. I wish I could get inside her head so that I could know how she feels about everything she has left. Her head, I am sure, is not a quiet place, either.

She knew nothing about hard work. I keep remembering this. Nothing – and I suppose she still knows nothing. All she was interested in was books: reading them and, so I was told, writing them. I do not know what all this is about, for I cannot read or write, do not have the letters. I am αγράμματη. What does she write about? What *use* is all this? My son seemed to be proud of her: I am not sure why.

I sit here wondering, watching the dying fire. We are dying together, the fire and I, I think suddenly, but it will die first. It comes to me, and perhaps I have been told, that she writes about our life here, about us. Ο καλός Θεός, the Good God, knows why, but it is just as well, if this is indeed so, that she does not know our secrets. We keep them, guard them fiercely, as is only natural and right.

What must it be like, to read and write? My father knew; my husband knew. My sons and daughters know, although the girls do as women should, and concentrate on housework and cooking and children. What does she write about? Does she write stories? I cannot imagine this. Stories are for telling. Aloud, with the voice. I was the one for telling stories, seated by this very fireplace. Everybody listened. Why should they not? Our lives are stories, after all. And what we want most is a good ending. With God.

The fire has gone out. There are only black coals on the hearth and blackness in the room. Everybody has gone and I have been put to bed. My last thought is: will I see the light again?

I r e n e In May of 1981 it became
obvious that I was pregnant with Joachim. I
rang my mother, who made noises like a dying
goldfish and then, she told me later, had the first of
many sleepless nights. The life sentence of mother-
hood.

Then the four of us set off on a brief holiday to the
Ionian island of Kefalonia.

May 1981

We broke the news to the boys while we were
away on Kefalonia last weekend. Thomas was
immediately delighted as he thinks babies are
'cute little things'. Michael was very sceptical.
His first comment was, 'You're fibbing.' His
second comment was, 'How do you *know*
you're going to have a baby?' But now he likes
the idea. The thought of a girl hasn't entered
their heads – they are assuming they'll have a
brother and are already debating the virtues of
names. Michael has washed his white teddy in
readiness.

It was difficult to be a modern woman. My sister-
in-law informed me in hushed tones that of course I
wouldn't be able to go swimming. I announced that of
course I would be going swimming. Yiayia looked the
other way. The local doctor declared that everybody

would be shocked and in any case I shouldn't go swimming after the sixth month. I said I didn't care whether they were shocked or not, and was determined to go swimming in a spirit of missionary zeal.

How important those efforts seemed then. Now nothing seems very important except the knowledge that my children, Joachim in particular, are happy.

The weather in Hampstead is awful, again. Of course one doesn't come to England for the weather, but the phone calls and letters of the last couple of days remind me of the clear heat of the Peloponnese. Thirty degrees is my favourite temperature; today, in the city of London, meteorologists predict a maximum of fifteen. Fifteen! Once again I will miss October in Greece – my month, with the little summer of Saint Dimitrios and its golden days and tawny chrysanthemums. What to do? When the practice of the noble art of distraction palls, what *is* there to do but sit and write endlessly to Joachim? Postcards and notes for letters.

I went out to post them this morning, steering my way carefully between sticky leaves, brown and yellow and faded now, gummed to a smeared pavement. I was feeling distinctly sun-starved until I realised that the charming Indian staff at the post office must suffer far more than I. Here in London Indian women wear saris in splendid, jewel-like colours and then have to put depressing layers of overcoats on top of them: the gold borders of their skirts are splashed with mud.

I sent Joachim a picture of Hampton Court and came back down Rosslyn Hill, where, to my very great surprise, I saw a bicycle almost entirely covered in strings and mesh bags of onions: the Kalamata market brought to Hampstead! The same sort of Greek confidence prevailed, too, for there was no onion vendor to be seen and it would have been very easy for any person to lift a string in passing. Thoughts of the disgrace of being caught, a middle-aged onion thief, saved me from temptation, kept me on the straight and narrow, so to speak, all the way home. That is, all the way back.

June and July of 1981 wore on. It was very hot, I did go swimming, and Michael fell ill. Then Australia Post went on strike for at least three weeks. I became maudlin with self-pity but kept on writing letters anyway, for the conversations in my head had to escape somehow, had to acquire some sort of reality.

Australia remained alive in Thomas and Michael's consciousness: they taught a neighbouring child to play cricket and kept their grandparents up to date with their doings and excursions. I bribed them to write postcards, strike or no strike, to do their correspondence lessons and to read; before the days of galloping inflation they received a drachma a page for Greek and two for English.

I was in despair over the postal strike, but despair is a pointless business because things keep changing all

the time. I hope the boys can remember this. Suddenly
the strike was over and, what was more, Hellenic Post
wrought a miracle. Deserving of libations it was, the
whole organisation, for delivering a letter addressed
thus (following my name):

School teacher
The village [*Messinias* had been added in Greek]
Near SPARTA
Southern Peloponnese
GREECE

My excitement at receiving a letter from a total
stranger was such that I made an utter hash of opening
the aerogramme. The letter brought news of an article
of mine that I didn't even know had been accepted.

> July 1981
>
> Your fine piece on migration and its effects on
> heart and mind and impulse to live . . . Here is
> my glass raised to your Statement, and my
> thanks to you for writing it . . . It's made my
> day.

The letter made my week, and it took about that
long for the grin to fade from my face. Vasili made all
the right noises but did not really understand. Nobody
could. It was as if somebody had moved a rock away

from the cave entrance, just a crack, and let in some heat and light. The concluding sentence let in more. 'What are you going to write next?'

That question meant a world, a future for me. It was an affirmation that I could keep going, even in the village where I was not competent and was always, I felt, on the wrong wavelength, able to communicate only by means of hammerlike blows instead of the feather-duster strokes I was used to. What I didn't realise at the time was that a split was opening in my life and in my consciousness. I was being fed by Greece and by Australia, yet I was effectively removed, by language and by distance, from both these places.

My correspondent was Amy, and it was so appropriate that she was an Englishwoman of Scottish extraction, older than I, who had lived in the Mediterranean and was now in Australia. Originally from Buckinghamshire, she visited Greece when she was nineteen and later lived in Spain. She *knew*.

My Australian generation, the Anglo-Celtic one, is the last of its kind. Thomas does not think of me as Australian; he has lived in Australia for four years now, and I am, he rightly maintains, very different from his Greek, Italian, Maltese and Vietnamese acquaintances and friends. At my mother's funeral there were ten different cultures represented, including the Laotian Chinese Buddhists from next door. There was standing room only on that occasion, for my mother was greatly loved, as she deserved to be.

It is also appropriate that I am here in England at this time in my life. There is a certain healing power here, despite my moans about the weather and a sensed, inevitable alienation connected with my childhood. When I was growing up, Australia and Britain interacted in a way which today's young find impossible to imagine. I could not decide during my childhood whether Australia was grafted on to England, or England on to Australia. That's the effect of being part of a transplanted culture, I suppose. Now I've come back to my roots, but the layers of top-dressing have, over the years, been sifted away.

All this will not make much sense to Joachim now. Perhaps it will later on: I want him to understand, eventually – and to know – this person who is his mother.

I replied to Amy's aerogramme immediately; her answer came as quickly as the combined efforts of Australia and Hellenic Posts permitted.

August 1981

Your letter arrived, which means my letter
arrived. I can't believe it. As I pulled it out of
the letterbox the wattle spilled pollen and
blossom on to it, and I felt on the threshold of
two worlds for a moment: my Mediterranean
one and my new Australian one.

Amy went on to say that she had Vegemite in the cupboard, one husband, one son and one cat, and I rather liked the order of her priorities. She also said, 'By letter you are already linked to me . . .' We have remained linked ever since. Joachim is linked to me, too, although he never writes, as is another person, who writes only seldom, very seldom. There are other links besides letters of course, but letters are a form of communicating in the beyond. I like that thought, which is not original. It is very hard, as Joachim will learn, to have an original thought.

Later Amy wrote about Joachim and his possible name.

September 1981

Your baby. Xenophon or whatever. How about Howzatt? It seems marvellous to have a baby, providing you have the strength to do the raising and enjoy it. That is the snag. I think grandmothers are mostly coined out of mothers who didn't have time to play with their own children, only time to look after them . . . A year ago I lost my mother . . . I lost my father a few months earlier, and my home in England, and my roots, and all this waited until the night of her death, then all the losses stacked. I ask you to imagine Greece without any Australian family here as a certainty. Suddenly the adopted land appears, despite love, a strange place, and life itself some form of forced exile. I am coming to terms with the lot, and life is beginning to grow again, but I am working quite hard to do it. My task is to celebrate the present fully, not defended from past pain but accepting it, having let it come through me without defiance.

On rereading this courageous letter, I am suddenly struck by the thought that I have two adopted countries, that my native land is no longer home to me. Bitter thought. Life as exile, indeed.

It was Amy who put me straight when I misquoted W. B. Yeats. Joachim is not yet thirteen; the quotation will not mean much to him and nor should it.

> Now that my ladder's gone
> I must lie down where all ladders start
> In the foul rag-and-bone shop of the heart.

I don't imagine he knows what a rag-and-bone shop is – may he never find out. As for his ladder, I'll keep it in place, keep propping it up, for as long as I can.

Joachim knows that Irene is a published writer and takes this fact for granted in a way she never can. What he does not know is that she is sometimes criticised severely for writing about her life. It seems that people do not always understand the compulsion, the pain, of writing, the need to sort things out. Irene's mother used to write letters to herself, trying to solve problems, deal with pain, sort things out on paper. After her mother's death, Irene found these letters and tore them up. Her letters to Joachim will be different: she hopes he will never tear them up.

J u l i e t   The classes have been better this week. It is strange how they improve, as life in general does if you just hang on and trust God that it will. We have to believe that everything, in teaching and life, turns out well in the end. I say we, but Irene obviously isn't one of us. Well, she is and she isn't.

She isn't, we think, because she writes about our lives. Most of us write letters: some of us keep our other writing to ourselves. We react to her writing; after all, she's using us, isn't she? The fact is, we're all foreign wives, we've all migrated and died the death that migration demands; we're all exiles and suffer the continuing pain of the divided heart. We could all write books.

I suppose I mustn't be over-sensitive and accusatory, for we all have to cope in our own way. Writing's her therapy; prayer's mine. Every night I pray for her to come back, to come home. She feels she doesn't belong, but does she belong anywhere? Do any of us, if it comes to that? Well, I feel I belong here now. It's taken me a long time to feel this way, but I've done it. Of course I'm not a complete fit, but I've handled things pretty well.

I don't know how Irene can manage without a home, really I don't. Her garden, for example; it was always hers, and now it's not the same at all. But she hasn't been able to stay away, and Joachim isn't the only reason for that, I'm sure. As she once missed Australia, she now misses Greece, I think. Perhaps she misses both places equally. It's hard to know. I can't imagine being in her situation. Surely one loyalty wins in the end? The heart decides.

I can't imagine, either, how she copes with missing Joachim, or with the thought of him missing her. Her feelings for him are different, she told me once. She nearly died having him and she said it was shocking to think she might never have known him. And then, two years ago, during the summer of her breakdown, he saved her life, kept her going, got her through it, she believes. She also believes that he understands her decision, her comings and goings. She's told him that she'll be back again before too long. He probably does understand in his way, and I don't think he blames her; he's not the type to blame anybody.

Even I, in my small way, know of the connection between writing and suffering. That's why I list my problems. Writing them out helps make them more manageable. Irene will be able to write much more now, and more than usual about herself, now that she's doing a fair imitation of an ageing princess wandering about in an impenetrable, endless forest.

Once she'd started writing, or rather publishing, for she told me that she has always written for herself, she wasn't going to stop. Writers' minds never switch off; writers never take holidays. I used to observe her observing: she's got a sharp eye for detail and nothing much ever got past her. I could almost see her thinking about the meaning of an incident and how she could use it. It's true there are some experiences we can't do anything about, but writers save them and then make something out of them. Lucky writers. Not so lucky writers. I know Irene very well, but in spite of my interest in writing I don't envy her the sheer restlessness of it, the rehearsing of phrases, of adjectives, the wondering how to combine things, the searching for the necessary angle from which to approach the subject matter, the hope that writing will somehow solve the problem. The worst part of all must be the constant reworking of the same material and the continual worry that all the drafts in the world are not going to guarantee *rightness*. Sometimes, she used to say, you have to give up or go mad.

'It's a mug's game,' she grinned ruefully once, sounding very Australian right then, 'but what is there to be done about it? It's an obsession, a virulent plague with no known antidote.'

We'd probably feel better if she wrote fiction. We used to joke and tell her to imitate Jeffrey Archer. 'Do you mind?' she would reply. 'He's strictly for the plot-addicted, although I confess to a deep envy of his royalties.' Some of us felt exploited, and muttered about ethics and morality, but what's truth, after all? Especially in writing – all that selection and shaping. It's hard to know. Anyhow, this whole business of giving anybody permission to be creative is a terribly tricky one.

That was yet another problem Irene had, I think. No permission, as such, was given her to write. Permission was given for teaching, an occupation people understand and which brings in a guaranteed, if small, income. Greeks, like everybody else, are very interested in money. It must be hard to keep working creatively when other people think your work isn't important or is just plain useless. She felt this, as she felt that she came first only with her children. And of course that doesn't last. Nor should it.

Writing made her life difficult. She might have been better off if she'd been able to sink uncritically into village life. Well, to be fair, very few of us can do that. But most of us can switch off to a certain extent and not worry about interminable weekends spent making tomato paste or soap. She couldn't. She was always worrying about meaning and shape, and was always aware of the swift passage of time, always had to be achieving something. I love her dearly, but she's ambitious.

The other thing is, she's always been in a good deal of emotional pain. We all are, that's a fact. Pain comes to everybody in the course of a lifetime but you positively invite it if you migrate. It's a knotty problem, the whole thing. Migration is a temptation at first: that sense of beckoning opportunity, the chance to reinvent yourself. But eventually the same distance that once enchanted begins to mock, and makes many a bad, sad situation much worse and much sadder. Who said you can burn letters and wish death, but the past is still the past? Sounds like something quoted by Irene. What do you think of *that*? Juliet, she'd say, I don't *want* to think of it, I'd reply, because I know that the person wrapped in those cocoon layers is still the same person. No bridge is ever really burned.

Irene's children are used to her talking to herself. She has done so for years. Like her mother before her. Once she used to sing to herself as well. Occasionally she still does, when she is out walking, when the sun is shining, when the sick feeling in her stomach goes away. Strange how the heart affects the stomach.

Irene thinks her heart is not tugged by Australia in the way it used to be, for she has been away too long and Australia is not the same. And her mother is dead. But this very day she was felled by the sound of 'The Wild Colonial Boy' being played on a piano accordion at King's Cross tube station. She almost stumbled off the escalator, then realised with a shock that she would probably now react to the sound of anything by Theodorakis and Hadzidakis in exactly the same way – here in London. For 'Zorba's Dance' and 'Giaconda's Smile' are part of her youth.

She has taken to writing in the tube. She is fascinated by the tube and cannot understand why people take it for granted, this concrete and steel metaphor for life with its subterranean interconnections and meshings, the importance of every cog and signal. She admires the brains and minds that conceived it, dreamed it and made it real.

For a long while after first coming to London she seemed to be the only one in all the tube crowds to sit and gaze. She noticed how most people were alone, how few of them talked, how nearly everybody was reading something: the various papers, Jeffrey Archer, Joanna Trollope. She saw a girl weeping copious tears once, with everybody pretending not to notice. Everybody except Irene, who was too far away to reach her or to do anything, and who did not know whether she was relieved or sorry.

Today she travels back to a summer long gone.

I r e n e   In this city where I least expected to live I think, not for the first time and not originally, how life is so much more and so much less than we expect. Experience jolts us from one place to another: this letter that I wrote in 1981 refers to something that took me to Australia in a most unexpected way.

August 1981

We have had a dramatic week here. Bushfires, no less! The mountains opposite were hidden by a thick pall of smoke. By 3 p.m. the church bells were ringing wildly – a tocsin, in fact. By this time the fire was threatening the next village and was less than a kilometre away. It seemed very close as I looked out of the bedroom window. Thomas was quite calm but Michael was terrified, and was not helped by stupid old women who were crossing themselves and saying, in peculiarly satisfied tones, 'Now we're going to burn, every one of us!' Michael wanted to return to wintry Australia immediately. Nobody had a clue

about fires. It was like a shaft of light when I
said that animals and people should go to the
river and cover themselves with soaked
blankets.

It was a nice change, feeling that I knew something
useful. At that stage, lonely and pregnant, I was feeling
swamped, particularly by the way in which the villagers felt free to give their unsolicited opinions about
absolutely everything, so that I felt like engaging in a
serious act of rebellion: calling the baby Jane, Eliza-
beth, Rufus or William. Something really English.
Where I was rebellious, Thomas was jittery.

Because Yiayia tells Thomas gory stories about
times past, he keeps asking whether the baby
is going to die or be peculiar, like one
specimen down the street. I try to be
sympathetic and reassuring but my patience
wears very thin. While Thomas worries about
the baby's demise, Michael worries about
mine!
   I think we have decided on Joachim John
in the event of a boy: suitably international.

The fit of rebellion passed and I got on with the
business in hand, which was looking after my children
and concentrating on getting a house built to put them

all in. Joachim and the house raced neck and neck and the end was more or less a dead heat; we moved in on his arrival in the village, even though the house was far from finished.

My faithful correspondents, and there were many of them, helped keep me going. Amy was constant in her support, sending me cuttings and thoughts about battling women, those who believed, as I still do, that they had to keep fighting.

'My only thought,' Amy wrote, 'is that of time. Time must come in fleeting quantities for writing with your multiple life.'

How right she was. Now I have so much time that I'm careless with it. I find myself thinking that there must be shirts and socks and meals to be attended to.

Two months before Joachim was born I started teaching English lessons in the village. This was a crazy thing to do, and thus typical, but I could no longer travel into Kalamata and we needed the money. I also needed something to do. Suddenly and surprisingly, Thomas and Michael wanted to learn English, too. Because they were native speakers it was an ego trip for them, but Thomas insisted on speaking English with a Greek accent until I was ready to throttle him.

I managed to keep writing to Amy, who wrote back and gave me lots to think about. She is still doing this.

October 1981

Children who disagree, argue, scoff, wrangle,
etc. are much more likely to become happier
adults than those who go neatly on their knees,
reverent and clean. But I do note, when men
speak of the importance for children of wearing
down the parental image from god to human,
they don't specify which parent gets most wear!

I found I could either bring up a baby or
read Spock. I couldn't face both and so I
chucked Spock.

Her letter reassured me as I alternated between
pre-operation nerves and the fatalistic calm I described
to my parents.

October 1981

We have to ring the doctor about ten days
beforehand to tell him, as Vasili cheerfully
puts it, to sharpen his knives. My brain is
moving into the placid, bovine state of the
last four pregnant weeks. All I can manage to
think about is my knitting and my hospital
case.

I have to confess that this placidity had disappeared by the time I was ready to go to Athens to await
Joachim's imminent arrival.

Children are not allowed to visit the hospital.
I am very disappointed. Thomas and Michael
are to stay in the village. My morbid streak
keeps on: they'll fall down wells, get run over,
choke on fishbones, get violently ill.

The little washing machine gave up the
ghost a month ago, so hand-washing is the
order of the day again.

I sometimes think I should have become a
career hermit. Solitude and a dark cave have a
distinct appeal.

Friend Helmut stopped just short of telling
me I'm mad. He says it's difficult enough to
live in 1981AD without regressing to BC with
donkey thrown in. Perhaps he has a point.

Vasili will be in touch as soon as possible.
Repeat: do not worry about delays.

In any idle moment I find myself going
calmly and resolutely into sheer panic. I only
hope that the doctor is as competent as he is
decorative. Vasili visited him in his Athens
surgery and said it was like a drawing-room,
with leather furniture and thousands of dollars
worth of modern art on the walls, and packed
to capacity with extremely wealthy-looking
Athenian females. So I suppose they must feel
he can cut straight and sew firm!

That trip to Athens in 1981 took place in the worst November weather anybody could recall. Vasili had to work and so I was on my own during the day. I wandered the streets of Ambelokipi near the Australian Embassy, bought and read thrillers and wrote letters in an effort to stop myself from jittering. In the event, I did not have to jitter for very long: Joachim, always impatient, decided to come early.

November 1981

Your new grandson is sleeping peacefully. He
is the image of Thomas and Michael, but
rather darker and with more hair, including an
apelike fringe on his ears. Like Thomas he is
an impatient and aggressive feeder.

I've had a very rough time: I'll write you all
the gory details later on . . .

I think Christmas will be in February this
year. I have missed you both dreadfully: not
improved by the hospital's initials of MMH
being embroidered on everything.

MMH were my mother's initials. I recently reread the follow-up letter, the one including the gory details, and could not believe that all that had happened to me, to us. How close I came to never even setting eyes on Joachim. The grimness of that thought!

At the age of thirty-six I wanted my mother so

155

badly that in the haze between sleeping and waking I occasionally thought she was in the room, and shed tears of disappointment on realising this was not so. I spent ten weeks in bed after I had Joachim, and thought I would never be properly vertical again.

Amy had told me not to stop writing whatever happened, but I was too exhausted and depressed to write anything except letters for a long time. While I was in hospital Australia Post went on strike again for what seemed like an eternity. Officials had to go round and seal up post-boxes that were full to overflowing, my mother told me later. But suddenly the strike was over – although Aristides the postmaster kept sending lugubrious messages about a Canadian postal strike that had lasted four months – and there I was, propped up by pillows, Joachim asleep beside me, with stacks of letters arriving and being read in the wrong order, strewn all over the bedspread.

December 1981

Thomas and Michael are delighted with Joachim, especially since he started smiling at eighteen days. He is now very alert and bright-eyed indeed.

My editor said I must be either very brave or mad. I wrote back and said I must be mad because I know I'm not brave.

While Vasili is at work I have to have the

baby in bed with me, thermos and bottles by the side of the bed, nappies at hand, etc. The boys, who are on holidays, are very good at fetching and carrying, but naturally I dare not let them lift Joachim out of his cradle. I must say he is being very good. I hope I don't have to go back to hospital.

My erratic handwriting became even more erratic as a result of writing in bed, and every so often a smear of milk or a dab of olive oil would find its way onto a page or two. My letters at this time, naturally enough, were almost entirely about Joachim and his brothers. Amy wrote that children are demonstrations of life in action, and that is indeed true, but I was becoming tired of my own enforced passivity. To which complaint Amy replied that Virginia Woolf said her best work was done when she appeared to do nothing. But I am not V. Woolf.

Nineteen eighty-two crept up on us: I wrote a New Year letter to my mother.

January 1982

There's absolutely nothing ennobling about pain, I've decided – it just makes me bad-tempered.

Joachim is F-A-T *fat*, and is becoming very sociable. He now has outsize dimples when he laughs. He's getting spoiled from being in bed with me all the time, but I don't see what else I can do.

Got supply of Vegemite. Put some in Joachim's bottle because Vitamin B is supposed to help eczema. His newborn darkness has faded and he's now quite fair-skinned. Vasili says that when he was born he looked Greek and now he looks foreign. Everybody says he looks like me. His hair has a touch of ginger about it, and occasionally he looks exactly like his Australian great-grandfather. That's not just my fond fancy, either, because Vasili noticed it first.

Thomas was fed up because Christmas was very dull: no toys. Michael told him not to mind. 'You're big now,' he said.

Wasting muscle: legs those of a seventy-year-old, and my bones are stiff.

Joachim screams blue murder and definitely has the huge lung capacity you would expect. Poor deprived child has been in an aeroplane but not in a pram as yet.

The fact that the new beginning of which Joachim was the symbol became an end so speedily had nothing to do with him. He is still at the stage now where time has no great significance: he looks on a pattern of school and holidays and trips abroad and visits from various people, and probably thinks, if he thinks about it at all, that it will last forever. And that is the way he should think. But I'll have to point out that in middle-age people suddenly realise that life is short. I'll try to explain all sorts of things to him, like the fact that I was raised a Puritan: yes, I'll use the capital P. Thus I believed in discipline and hard work, the stripping away of comfort, which was too much like self-indulgence, and frugality. How else could I have managed in the village? But my pioneer soul believed in progress as well, and thought that virtue and persistence would eventually have their reward. I tried to do all the right things; I tried to be the essence of sweetness and light, but often became exhausted and irritable and not at all nice to be near instead.

In my late middle-age, after years of sitting on straight-backed chairs, I wanted to sink onto a chaise longue. I longed for comfort and ease but lost any semblance of security instead. What I believed was certainty turned out not to be. How greatly I had confused my perceptions with reality. I had continually allowed my fatal imagination to persuade me that I was loved. I had willingly, eagerly even, closed my eyes to the fact that I was not. It was hard for me to accept Vasili's indifference and his family's lack of interest in me and my situation, but eventually – and how long it took! – I realised that they simply did not care. I had built an absolute trust on foundations which proved to be very shaky indeed.

I tried too hard and hoped for too much: people can only be, after all, what they are. I was naïve in that I believed that everything would be all right in the end. In the end, all I had was a yawning gap of loss and very little with which to plug that gap. Neither do I have a sense of direction; I am, quite simply, lost.

Sometimes Irene feels she is Penelope to Vasili's Odysseus. His future was his past, his Australian life merely a long dream of home in a mainland Ithaca. Returning there, he found not his wife but his mother, as he remembered her, at her loom, still weaving the old patterns that he had never forgotten. She, rather than the Australian Penelope he had brought with him, was the expert, although Penelope did her best in her clumsy way.

But Penelope eventually became weary of weaving and waiting. Her heart wasn't in the unravelling; she wanted to move on. She wanted the future to be the future, not the past. She wanted adventure and travel and fun and companionship, for she believed in recompense for hard work, and she certainly knew a great deal about that.

Make no mistake: she wanted these things with

Odysseus for a very long time. But Odysseus was not interested. She begged and cried but he would not listen. Then she began to cry inside, and to go away a lot, to keep herself to herself.

Odysseus was a wily character who got what he wanted. He managed to come back home; Penelope lost not just one but two homes. And stopped weaving.

I r e n e   Things did get better before they got worse. I made the big announcement to my parents after what seemed like a lifetime of invalidism.

February 1982

I am *up!* And am having predictable problems
with Joachim. After spending weeks in bed
with me, he naturally fails to understand why
I have to disappear in the direction of the
washing machine or elsewhere. He still
resembles the Buddha and is growing very
fast.

Some spring flowers have already started
to appear.

I had been on my feet a fortnight when my parents arrived for a stay of three months. I stood shaking on the platform at the railway station and then had to walk away from them lest I break down completely. They came, they saw, and they managed everything, a fact for which Vasili, who was also exhausted, and I were devoutly thankful. The house was put to rights, the garden tamed, set out and laced with paths.

We did things, always in the company of Joachim. We went to Pylos and Methoni, to ancient Ithome and into Kalamata, and up to the *plateia* where we saw a play about which I remember nothing, most likely because I understood not a word of it.

It is strange how difficult it is now to recall the spring of 1982 – perhaps a result of illness, convalescence, and a general letting-go which happens, even in maturity, when your parents are on the scene. My parents were very young when I was born. They were more extroverted than I; it seemed to me, even as recently as 1982, that they were people of great energy, dash and power. All they had to do was to apply their superior intelligence and steely will, which they had in great abundance, to any problem and that problem would be solved. So it seemed, and now I realise how young I was still, in that spring. I let go gratefully and tried not to think of summer.

Joachim was a *bon bibeur* and a *bon viveur* – I remember that well enough – a foodie of only a few months. He was a butter-ball who shook with desire at the sight of a bottle of milk; he grunted and sighed with pleasure, his toes curled in ecstasy. My father said we should attach him by hose to a tanker of milk and leave him to it. He was a podge so fat that his legs, like those of his mother and brothers before him, became bandy as soon as he started to walk: like a cowboy in miniature, except that his pony was missing.

Yes, we were both young then. Ten years later, again in the spring, I realised I was not young any more. Life had taken me by the throat and threatened to strangle me.

After her mother died Irene went back to Australia and had an extra summer, during which she felt at once ancient and like a child in the front line when the big guns have stopped firing. She travelled to Dimboola through landscape she had not seen for nearly forty years. She had been younger than Joachim is now when she last saw that place of red earth and large blue skies which are not much cluttered by hills and mountains.

At Dimboola Irene stood at the crossroads, where one road curved back to Pimpinio, and signposts pointed to Adelaide, Jeparit and Warracknabeal. It was a displaced person who stood and gazed and took a personal inventory: Greek jeans, jumper and shoes bought in Edinburgh, shirt borrowed from her sister, socks bought at a stall in the Portobello Road. It was symbolic, she thought, that her underwear was Australian.

She was eleven when she last saw this place. Then her mother was with her and then nobody had thought of writing a play called *Dimboola*. Now her mother is dead and Irene, standing there at the crossroads, is wearing her mother's watch and wedding-ring and nobody else's.

Just before leaving Australia she dreamt she was in a jewellery shop where she bought only one of a pair of earrings in the shape of Australia. She placed it in her ear and promptly fell over, took it out and straightened up immediately.

I r e n e   In the spring of 1982 my parents returned to their own place and I started writing to them again.

June 1982

Last week Kalamata was the hottest place in Greece with a temperature of 45°. One sunflower is now as tall as I am. Yiayia's donkey ate all the grass, so the place is a bit tidier.

Beach: after a quarter of an hour spent

meditatively chewing on large pebbles,
Joachim was initiated into swimming. He took
to the water like the proverbial duck.

Now there is no four-legged lawnmower but this
year Joachim and I counted twenty-nine buds on the
summer sunflower.

Later in 1982 I met a Greek professor and his
French wife, who was like a tonic. Tall, elegant and
encouraging, she praised my Greek and remarked carefully on the differences between Athenian and village
life. She appeared completely her own person. French
poodle tucked under one arm, she strode into the
kafeneion and demanded a saucer of lemonade for it.
Lemonade! Vasili, who was in the *kafeneion*, thought
that the old men would faint with horror. Enjoying
himself hugely, he proceeded to tell them at great
length and in precise detail about a poodle parlour
near our house in Melbourne, and how the pampered
pooches would be delivered there for sessions of shav-
ing, dyeing, and toenail clipping. One ancient, par-
tially deaf and as blind as a bat, did not follow
spectacle or narrative at all.

'What's that she's holding?' he demanded as the
poodle, drink over, was tucked under its owner's arm
again. 'A newfangled handbag?'

I laughed but it was not long before self-pity
caught up with me again.

August 1982

One of my problems in Greece, I've decided,
is wounded ego. Not very nice to know about
oneself, but it's true. The other problem is that
I can feel my brain rusting and I'm getting out
of touch with the rest of the world.

I am hurrying to catch the post. Have just
discovered that the water will be off again
between 2 and 6 p.m.

Oliver Sacks has said that each of us is a singular
narrative. 'To be ourselves, we must have ourselves –
possess, if need be re-possess, our life stories. We must
"recollect" ourselves, recollect the inner drama, the
narrative of ourselves.'

I see now the storyline that I wrote for myself:
handsome prince, faraway land, sweet and pretty girl,
happy ever after. The real plot was not at all like that,
and at a deep and often repressed level I rebelled,
although the bubbles of rebellion took a long time to
work their way to the surface and erupt.

One Lenten night long ago, Yiayia and her eldest
daughter told me about the egg custom: you place
eggs on the hearth and if they do not sweat it is a por-
tent of disaster. Yiayia's mother did this once, Yiayia
told me tensely, and one egg broke, then disappeared.
No trace of it remained, and not long afterwards
Yiayia's eldest brother died.

I left, I remember, before they could do the egg test on me. I really did not want to know if mine remained cool and composed. My empty Turkish coffee cups used to show lots of little lines, straight and wavy. Travel, said the old *yiayiáthes*, shaking their heads, plenty of travel. They were right, although it took me a while to get started. Now it seems difficult to stop. I keep on the move in order to avoid wearing out my various welcomes, and in order to keep worry and too much thought at bay. My mother considered I thought too much and said so. It was a habit I couldn't break. Writing seems to be another.

In that summer of 1982 Joachim still resembled Michelin Man, so that the priest had his hands full during the christening. The christening notice appeared in the local paper. Vasili's name also appeared – mine did not. In August there was a mouse plague and I found a furry corpse under Joachim's cot; the washing-machine thought seriously about giving up the ghost, and the flue of the wood stove collapsed, showering everybody and everything in soot.

But Joachim was all right. He seemed to have quite a good time, despite the irritations of being a baby. I kept his doting grandmother up to date.

August 1982

He now has six teeth and I'm paying for every one of them. He's the village rock star. He

dances madly to anything and has the most
flexible knees in the Peloponnese. He even
dances when he hears the church bells;
perhaps he thinks he's a Hasidim and not
Greek Orthodox.

I don't think his ginger hair will last, as his
eyelashes are long and dark. Pity. He certainly
looks a true Scot at the moment: eyes more
grey than green and his skin quite fair. I think
he has fined down in the thigh but not in the
middle.

He's taken as many as ten steps but is
rather chicken about going any further, or else
gets so excited that he falls in a heap. I've had
to tie the cupboard doors up . . .

The following autumn was rather grim, as I recall.
Vasili went away on business and returned an exhausted
bundle of nerves after waking up on consecutive days in
Trier, Paris, Luxembourg, Frankfurt, then home. I was
too weary even to be jealous, had shingles, refused to
leave the house, and rather felt as if I should have had
a little bell like the ones the lepers were compelled to
carry in the Middle Ages. Joachim's good time ended
when he and his brothers contracted chicken pox one
after the other. Then Vasili succumbed as well.

A r t e m i s   Late afternoon. Joachim is here. They all think that I am very much alone but that is not true, for the spirits of my dead visit me. And my sons and daughters are always coming and going. They, my children, are either afraid of finding me dead, or they are hoping, for I have lived too long. But at this moment Joachim is here and that is the main thing.

He is sitting quietly. He talks to me often, but at this minute I am sitting with my eyes closed and he believes I am asleep. I do not sleep as much as people ⟨ suppose. It is much easier to think while my eyes are closed.

He is a beautiful boy, Ιωακείμ. He has my eyes. In fact he is very much like us, there is very little of the foreigner in him at all. The good God knows what He is about. He was a fat, spirited baby – a true Greek. Our name is not wasted on him.

I open my eyes to look at him and at once forget my last thought. He smiles. With me he does not worry about showing his teeth, which now have squares and strips of metal on them. I smile back and do not worry either, even though I have no teeth at all. He does not seem to mind. He does not flinch away, even though I am not a pretty sight. I was once, and I have to be content with that knowledge.

Joachim. What was I thinking about? Oh yes. Before his birth I never mentioned anything about a baby coming. That would have been foolish. Very foolish. The Evil Eye would have done its worst. Only the good grace of Η Παναγία, the All-Holy one, and a merciful God protected Joachim. I am certain of that. The things his mother was doing at the time – may all the saints watch over us. She went swimming. I was ready to die of shame but held my head high, which is the only thing to do when circumstances, people and the fates are against you. Then she only had two months to go when she started giving English lessons in the *sala* upstairs. All the ragtag and bobtail came, children whose parents are not worth considering. Why some people do not know their station in life is beyond me. Of course some respectable children also came, I cannot deny that. And she was earning money. But teaching in the *house*. Schools are the places for teaching.

My thoughts are in order now, at least for the moment. Teaching in the house went on for a long time. In her house. She wanted her own house and she got it. My son would have been quite happy to stay here with me. It is cheap living here, and it is the house he grew up in. It is his place. I myself did not really want to leave my father's house either, because it was my place, but that is what women have to do. I was given a husband and parents-in-law and so I changed places, but only, it must be said, in a small way.

The new house was not enough, could not work a

miracle, could not, it seems, make the foreign *nifi* happy. But you are bound to be miserable when you are not even in your own country, you are bound to be. Then, I suppose, things went wrong between her and my son. I suppose so, I have never asked. Why would I? Whatever the problems were, she was a foolish, soft-hearted stubborn girl. You do not let men make you miserable. What would be the point of that? There is enough misery in life without allowing that to happen.

Joachim. His birth, they told me, was dreadful. The Evil Eye did not fail to do its work. Of course not. The baby was a fine healthy one but his mother nearly died. She fought for her life with great and silent determination, I learned, but lay in bed for nearly three months afterwards with Joachim beside her. She fought for her life as she later fought me over the baby's names. She was not much of a fighter, had no spirit, as I keep remembering, but she fought me over this. Well, in her fashion. She looked at me in her straight way and tried to speak as correctly as she could, taming her accent. 'You must permit me to name one child. He is the last I will ever have. My father has no one else to bear his name. And these are not foreign names: they are, both of them, Orthodox.'

She had her victory. I told her, and I hoped it would prove to be the case, that the priest would make trouble, would not give the child two names. But for once I was wrong. Old Papayianni had a soft spot for her, Heaven only knows why, and raised not a murmur. He had already forbidden me to take Ιωακείμ to church on the fortieth day when the *nífi* was still in bed. 'We will wait until the mother is better,' he said. I remember all that very well. I was angry. What about the child? I thought, but said nothing. However unsatisfactory some priests are, they still must be shown respect. 'The poor little thing,' he added, referring to the mother, not the baby. Poor little thing. Men. Men and their λόγια, their words, their odd mixture of softness and harshness.

I sit here with Joachim beside me and I think of all that has gone before, of birth and the threat of death and the clash of wills. Of Joachim growing steadily and bravely, of loss and of absence. His mother is still not here. But I am. I open my eyes to look at him. He smiles again. <<Εντάξει, Γιαγιά;>> he asks. 'Are you all right, Yiayia?' I nod. Yes, I am all right. I am always all right when you are here, παιδάκι μου, my little child. My eyes close again on this thought, but I say nothing.

J u l i e t It's Saturday night, a very quiet one. I love October: the softness of it, the run of sunny days, the Little Summer of Saint Dimitrios with its bursts of chrysanthemums and the rose light in the evenings. Soon little plumes of

172

smoke will start to rise in the light as the evenings draw in and become cooler. But here tonight it's still quite warm. I'm alone, writing. Pavlos is at the *kafeneion*; at least he said that was where he was going. But I don't really care where he is. Not any more. Joanna is fast asleep, I've just looked in on her.

Joachim's been here for most of the day. I suppose this friendship will change soon, because everything changes, nothing stays the same, but right now the children have a warm companionship which I envy. One mustn't envy the young, though. Envy doesn't do, and who knows what lies ahead of them?

The children's foreignness, perhaps, comes out in this easy friendship. Joachim treats Joanna, at least so far, as an equal and she shows him no deference at all, thank God. Today they've listened to their heavy-metal tapes, done their homework, gossiped about their classmates and teachers, and squabbled mildly about the football and volleyball competitions. Fortunately Pavlos and Vasili agree about politics. Of course they're distantly related, but that doesn't always matter in a country which has been through a bitter civil war.

The children talk in Greek between themselves, naturally, but they and I speak English together. This is what I've always done, because I've wanted to. It's unnatural, after all, to speak to a child in a language not your own. And now I think that this is something I can do for Irene while she's away. She too always spoke English to her children. Old Artemis resented it bitterly, couldn't bear the thought of people slipping beyond her control. That made Irene determined to keep it up, of course. She had to have some independence, and speaking English and writing were the only ways she could get it. She didn't negotiate, just asserted herself, did these things, grabbed at these areas because she had to. Language and communication were her professional *things*, and also part of her self: she hated making mistakes or expressing herself clumsily in Greek, simply hated it. We all inevitably go through that but some of us suffer more than others along the way.

It's clear that Irene and her departure have become an obsession with me. I sit here night after night thinking on paper. The more I do this, the more doomed her Greek venture seems to me to have been, even from the beginning. It was bound to end in tears, for all sorts of reasons, some of which I've already thought about for a long time.

The list of problems is endless. She didn't come first with anybody, was nobody's preferred company. She needed to be loved, for that's the way she is, but she wasn't. Her children adored her and still do, but that's different. She wanted a companion. What's the word? A soul-mate. Yes, that's what she wanted. I have no idea whether she's found one, as there's still no mention of a man in her life, but I occasionally think about the possibility and wonder whether she's had a disappointment.

Signals get mixed, often, I think, and mixed signals lead to trouble. Some people are like lighthouses. Their bright, regular flash can provide a sense of comfort during a storm, can be a compelling attraction to those who, like Irene, are adrift and searching for a safe harbour. But the flash is completely automatic and can also be read as a warning. Danger. Rocks ahead. Keep Your Distance.

Perhaps Irene set her sights on a signal like that, misread it and drove straight onto a reef? I don't know. But a great many men do not play fair, later expressing surprise that their simple friendliness has been taken the wrong way.

People can't give you what they haven't got. I learned that lesson with Pavlos, but I'm not sure whether Irene ever learned it with Vasili. He hurt her deeply in all sorts of ways, and I'm sure never realised what he was doing most of the time. People aren't all the same: sensibility, sensitivity, the imaginative leap aren't among the virtues of the older Greek male. I've greater hopes of the younger generation, though.

Irene is a woman acquainted with grief. It's easy to declare that what's gone and what's past help should be past grief. I haven't read any Shakespeare since school but I remember that. The whole idea turns on the word 'should', surely? I don't know that grief is ever past.

Irene and I are both, at this point, grieving for our lost youth, among other things, but I've stayed put with mine. Irene took hers and ran away. It's not clear to me what she's done with her bag of hopes and dreams. It's probably fallen apart in the streets of London, the contents scattered all over those hard pavements. She told me once that her family's motto is 'all or nothing'. She's certainly lived by it. I wonder if she's yet reached the conclusion that she could end up with nothing.

She wanted a different life, that was the thing. She wanted a literary sort of life in another place. Perhaps she felt that her life, her self, had been confiscated. Self. Place. Place is so important, as every *dis*-placed person knows. Places can hurt you, just as much as a heedless or vindictive person can, and it's obvious that the interaction of person and place can do a whole lot of damage.

Greece wasn't what Irene was used to, not what she wanted, and she didn't choose to be here. She came and stayed because she loved Joachim's father very much for a very long time. She told me that. I haven't, as I've said, ever visited Australia but Irene tells me everything's reversed there, in ways Europeans never dream of. Trees have dark foliage and light trunks, for example: it's like looking at the negative of a photograph. And Australia's certainly not Britain in the sun, so she says. Even visual adjustments are difficult, but she made all sorts of adjustment – or so it seemed. We both love Greece, God help us.

But it doesn't matter how much you love a new place, it is quite possible to be overwhelmed by a return to a familiar one. The longer you look forward to this return, the worse the reaction is likely to be. I've felt it myself on my rare returns to London. A lid has to be very firmly put on those feelings, otherwise they boil over. I keep the lid on. Irene was able to do the same, she said, during her visits to Australia. It was her visits to Britain that did the real damage. This was something I couldn't understand. Well, how could you expect to? she asked me. You're not Australian, not an Australian born at the very end of the last war.

She tried to explain how Britain – and this was hard for me to grasp – was for her familiar before being seen, before she got there. She *felt* it, she claimed, in the blood, because of the transplanted culture, the race-memories, the nostalgia transmitted from pioneer ancestors, and because of the unquestioning willingness, so much a part of colonial history, to fight for a place unseen. Joachim's Australian great-grandfather volunteered for Gallipoli. He hesitated too long though, and the famous evacuation took place while he was still somewhere on the high seas. He found himself in France and Belgium and took part in all the famous battles: the Somme, Vimy Ridge. Passchendaele, St Souplet, all these and more, and I probably haven't got them in the right order. It was four years before he saw home and mother again. What an awful thought: he risked everything he had every day for four years. Migration is bad enough, but not the same, not at all.

Anyway, this thing of feeling before seeing turned out to be quite important for Irene. Piccadilly Circus, for example. She'd seen a postcard of it when she was four, sent by her grandfather. 'I don't expect you to understand,' she said to me, 'but it meant a lot, the thought that Grandfather had stood where I was standing, looking at silvery Eros under a fickle sky. All that time ago. I can't explain what or how I felt. My grandmother never got there and never expected to.'

'Expectations,' she said to me. 'Now, there's a topic. Where do expectations come from? Who makes the promises? The old women here expect their reward in Paradise.' As for myself, I don't expect anything now. Remember Kazantzakis? «Δεν ελπίζω τίποτε». 'I hope for nothing'. Irene told me that in a resigned sort of manner, and then she repeated, 'Well, anyway, I can't explain what or how I felt the first time I stood in Piccadilly Circus.' How she felt. Feeling. She's a *feeling* creature. It hasn't done her much good. Not much good at all. But we are what we are and we do what we have to do. And now I must go to bed. Alone.

◎◎

Like most mothers, Irene is aware that part of her consciousness is alway tuned to her children. Even though her two eldest boys have grown into men who tower over her, they will always be her babies. Irene fears she will hate Thomas's and Michael's wives, although so far she has liked their girlfriends. She misses them when they vanish and they do not vanish willingly, a fact which makes Irene feel for them more, for she knows about broken hearts, considers herself something of an expert on unrequited love. She will hate Joachim's wife most of all. All the little things she takes note of in London, the trivial incidents she hopes might amuse and entertain him, give him a view of a different world, are an appeal to her absent child. I haven't forgotten you, they cry. Please don't forget me.

I r e n e   Joachim danced through the autumn of 1982. By then he had learned to dance *à la grecque*, with his hands held aloft. He danced whenever the mood, his κέφι, took him. He also sat in on, even before his first birthday, the English lessons I was giving at home. The letters, as usual, bring everything back.

October 1982

He's so good a dancer that I'm going to flog him out to work in a taverna. He wrinkles his nose when he laughs and tilts his head back as Greeks do instead of saying no. His first word is English – a victory for Mum! He waves Thomas and Michael off to school each morning and says ta-ta quite clearly. He 'reads' books constantly and burbles to himself, with his little index finger pointing out this or that.

He sits up at the table with his mouth open like a baby bird, although I don't think baby birds smack their lips in anticipation.

Nothing much is happening here. I'm very busy with the teaching; my beginners are madly keen and are all lovely children. One is called Euridice; all we need is an Orpheus.

Thomas and Michael were forced to plod away at their English lessons in addition to their ordinary homework because I insisted. All this, and my other teaching, took time, so that I was moaning yet again that I had hardly lifted a pen in four weeks and that the house looked like a second-rate brothel.

My love/hate relationship with the local school continued, and lasted through Joachim's time there, too. The teachers were very affectionate towards the children, and interested in them, but very set in their opinions. Thomas's teacher considered cards the Devil's playthings; he also announced that the new priest had a piece, presumably small, of the One True Cross. Bucking again at the feeling that I was living in some sort of medieval time warp, I announced that I was going to sell indulgences in the village square.

'What are indulgences, Mum?'

Little things, however, continued to delight me, as they still do. In the house of old Maria, our neighbour, my parents' photograph was propped against a vase of purple, orange and green zinnias, those stiff, layered circles that are so well-suited to Greece. Alongside the photo was the card my parents had sent her, upside down. Maria could not read at all – perhaps the English letters looked more comprehensible that way.

Panayioti the saddler made a most beautiful donkey saddle, commissioned by an Australian woman. He was so delighted at the thought of exporting it that he included an exquisite set of harness in the packing case. The woman lived in country Victoria where she bred donkeys and other animals; my brother bought his pet goat from her. When he went to collect it, there was a wallaby and an assortment of hens making themselves at home in the kitchen. The donkey saddle duly arrived and was the first that Melbourne customs officials had had to deal with.

One day, driving to Kalamata, we saw an old man wobbling along on a decrepit bicycle. He wobbled even more dangerously when he crossed himself as he passed a wayside shrine. I laughed – he would undoubtedly have blamed the Devil had he fallen off.

But there are quaint aspects to life in Hampstead, too. It's hard to stop looking out of the window. Today a pale weak sun is shining, and two Moslem women, each wearing the chador, one black and one purple, walk down the street carrying a chest of drawers. And there are bag-ladies in the district, two of them. One is very large and goes up and down Hampstead High Street, stopping for a rest in Barclays Bank or the post office, or pausing briefly on a seat to feed the pigeons. The other is much smaller and favours Belsize Park. She sits, talking to herself, surrounded by her bags and bundles, on the low wall outside what used to be the Town Hall. What happens to them at night, I do not know. They do not appear angry or resentful, but the smaller one appears to be in very frail health. They are both quite old. And winter is coming on, much faster than it does in Greece. Joachim doesn't know about bag-ladies; he knows only about gypsies.

Outside the light slants through foliage, patching and dappling the paved gardens which are edged with the delicate greenery called babies' tears, which grows in Australia but not, I think, in Greece. It tufts every crack, this little plant. Blackbirds and robins peck on the lawn. A furry tail flicks in a tree and for an instant I do not know where I am. I assume it is a possum. It isn't, of course; it is a grey squirrel and the owner of the house complains bitterly about it, for it eats fruit from the trees at a rapid rate.

The family with whom Irene stays in Hampstead employs an old cleaning lady, Mrs Behan, who has worked for them for thirty years. She rules with a rod of iron and has decided that Irene is a servant, too: it is definitely a case of Them and Us. Mrs Behan gives Irene the low-down on the household; Irene helps her fold sheets and straighten rugs and admires the spirit with which she leads her solitary life: she is a childless widow. Pride and solitariness have a strong appeal for Irene, the gregarious loner.

Irene knows little and can learn less about Mrs Behan. She assumes she lives in a council flat; she knows about the Catholicism and permits herself a grin when Mrs Behan sniffs and announces that converts are the worst. Mrs Behan goes to Mass on Sundays; she prays for various people, particularly mothers. Irene loves her for that alone.

Mrs Behan has her friends and they move routinely up and down Haverstock Hill on their way to the post office and the supermarket. She gives little boys 20p coins for sweets. Irene comes to know most of these friends and begins to feel herself, in a slight way, to be a member of a community.

Irene finds in Mrs Behan somebody she can recognise, for Mrs Behan is Irish and has the same lack of longing and yearning which was such a comforting part of the personalities of Irene's grandmothers and great-aunts. They were absolutely certain and confident about everything, this Celtic tribe of elderly females. They knew where they were; they knew where they were going. Money isn't everything, Mrs Behan, who hasn't any either, tells Irene. All we need is enough to eat and drink, a roof, and God's good grace.

I r e n e   Today I'm pottering about with Mrs Behan, whom Joachim would love; he would find her as entertaining and as spirited as I do. I took to her at once, even though her opening words startled me.

'Mind you remember everything you've been told about locks and keys, else everybody'll be murdered in their beds!'

She bosses me about. 'You're not eating properly. Where's the food in the fridge? Look after yourself. Drink that wine, I would. It'll only go off.'

She teaches me the fearlessness, the social fearlessness, of growing old. She watches soap operas and scatters cigarette ash on the carpets she has just cleaned. She primps in the mirror. 'Me hair's a disgra-ace. Must get to a hairdresser.' She gives me fashion advice. 'I do like your red cardigan. As we get older we need bright colours, don't we?' Thirty years divide us but I nod meekly in agreement.

She always has opinions and does not care how

they are received. A scion of a famous house comes to call and Mrs B shakes her head mournfully. 'Look at her,' she booms to me. 'Poor thing. Not at all like her parents.' She has a great sense of humour and immense charms, but Mrs B is not impressed. On another occasion: '*Three* husbands a certain person has had,' she announces darkly, naming a name. 'Isn't one enough, for t' love of God?'

Mrs Behan tells her surrogate family precisely what she thinks. She nags, scolds and complains and they beam lovingly upon her. She is like the Greeks, I will tell Joachim, in that she believes in righteous indignation.

'Do you know what that man, that electrician, asked me? He asked me if I was from Limerick. Limerick!'

'What did you say?'

'I said I'm from Cork, of course. Humph.'

'Where's he from?'

'Wales. I *knew* he was Welsh the first time he came.'

It is hard to convey the disdain with which she uttered the word 'Welsh'. She reminds me of an old Scot I knew once. I asked him what the Scots thought of the Welsh. 'Not much,' was the succinct reply. It's as bad as the Sydney–Melbourne rivalry, this tradition, and rather older.

We discuss weighty matters, Mrs Behan and I. Broken hearts, the nature of love. How Girls Should Behave. These subjects, and others, engage our attention. 'Broken hearts are just awful,' I state gloomily to her. 'I can't stand the idea of broken hearts, let alone the reality.'

'The young have to get over all that,' says Mrs B in her overalls, flicking the feather duster rhythmically. But it is not the young I am thinking of.

When I return to Greece she misses me, and I miss her. There is nobody to tell me to take an umbrella, to make sure I'm wearing a thermal vest. She even admires my Akubra hat.

Shortly after Joachim's first birthday we went to Athens, all of us, for a few days. It was eleven months and three weeks since I had been there and it was quite miraculous to be in a big city after all that time – the sense of excitement, the notion of things happening, of endless possibilities, of life expanding rather than contracting. Athens dances to a frenetic rhythm of its own. The rhythms of London and Melbourne are quite different, much more sedate.

I'm not sure whether Joachim has studied Pindar yet, or whether he knows that to him Athens was 'a divine city, shining and violet-crowned'. Joachim certainly knows about the *néfos*, the pollution cloud; now the only shine is on the surface of petrol spills, and the violet crown has been replaced by a muffling headscarf of black haze. In the autumn sunlight of our visit aristocratic women of a certain age, pale-faced, wrinkle-free, paraded furs and coiffures up and down Vassilisis Sofias.

But when buses belched vapour leaden in colour and content, silk handkerchiefs emerged from handbags, and mouths and noses were screened from the fumes. Nothing much had changed. It still does not do to think about the colour of one's lung linings and mucous membranes when in Athens, and, anyway, one needs to concentrate on one's splitting headache instead.

We went to the hospital again. The doctor was very pleased to see Joachim, although he considered him too fat. Joachim burst into tears at the sight of his beard and moustache. At Syntagma Square we fed the pigeons, and Joachim had his photo taken by American tourists who pronounced him 'a little doll'. I didn't want to leave Athens, its comforts, its modernity, the multitude of stimuli. As the years passed, I went there more and more often, and so did Joachim.

Back home in the village, Christmas was drawing near. It was freezing in the Peloponnese: knifelike winds howled day and night. Australia, predictably, was enduring drought. Christmas in Greece tended to be difficult, because of my home-thoughts from abroad, but I tried not to let the children see this. My mother's birthday fell three days before Christmas. I rang the family, I'm not sure from where. Although we had put in an application for a phone before Joachim was born, it was not connected until after his eighth birthday, so ringing entailed effort. But of course it was worth it.

On Christmas Eve Joachim fell flat on his face off

the front doorstep and as a result looked like a wounded warrior, with scraped cheek and forehead. Perhaps because of this I remember nothing of Christmas Day. But I can remember how jealous I felt when Amy's description of her Melbourne Christmas arrived.

December 1982

Streams of presents (gold, silver, black) piled
up in front of a whitewashed wall. We had
Christmas dinner in absolute bliss of an
Australian day of sunlight. We started with –
do you mind the flesh-pots? – smoked salmon,
and then wandered in the garden and returned
to have a roasted fillet steak (an hour in the
oven, the centre red for those who wished it,
the ends more done), and then after another
pause fresh peeled lychees and blueberry tarts.
Hours later, tea and tiny, individually wrapped
Christmas cakes tied with scarlet ribbon. I
gave a mid-17th-century grey Ming dish (also
tiny) to my son-in-law and to my daughter
something from my past – my great-aunt's
ruby earrings, surrounded by little seed pearls
in gold.

It all seemed so impossibly rich, elegant, carefree, and above all comfortable. *She* hadn't seen Yiayia's turkeys tied to a stake for a month before Christmas. I envied Amy her life, although I knew I'd chosen mine. We all have to choose. Juliet, for example, chose to live in Greece and chooses either not to see or not to think about Pavlos's infidelities. Isn't she hurt, though? I often wonder. Isn't she eaten up with jealousy at the thought of his body meeting someone else's, of the intimacy of it? It's all very well for men to say that infidelity doesn't mean a thing. To many women it means the whole world. Many women, and I am one, think the world well lost for love – but not for love's betrayal.

Joachim grew, sometimes slowly, sometimes in leaps and bounds, through the next decade. His own pattern evolved: chatty and voluble at home, a quiet observer in social situations. He really only spoke English with me and would beat me to the making of certain announcements: 'Thank God it's Friday,' he would say with a world-weary air as the last student disappeared at 9 p.m. 'Now I can have a little rest.' 'I'm not impressed,' he said firmly when something displeased him, and he was often displeased. His grandfather upset him once, during a holiday visit. Joachim, at the age of five, looked his ancestor in the eye and said grimly, 'I'll be glad when there are no old men about.' The thought was not mine but the manner of expression was.

There were periods, naturally, during which Joachim drove his brothers absolutely mad. He interfered, wanted to be with them, tagged after them when they least wanted him, fiddled with their things, drew all over their homework, flew into operatic rages, and cried a lot. But time changes all things and eventually Thomas was able to say, 'At some stage Joachim became human. He became, well, *reasonable*. I never thought he would.' I remember that I once thought Thomas never would, either.

Between them, Vasili and Irene opened up different worlds for their sons. It has been said that it is essential to remain loyal to one's beginnings. Irene envied Vasili because he never had any difficulty in this regard, while she cannot think that she is being loyal to hers.

Irene wonders about this question of loyalty, particularly in the middle of the night when it occurs to her that perhaps she is loyal after all, that the hundred and fifty years since her ancestors' migration have been some sort of historical hiccup and her spirit has, in some peculiar way, forced her body back to their older beginnings. She is not sure, but then Irene is not sure of anything much.

She was sure, briefly, once, when she found what she wanted very late and very unexpectedly. It was quite terrifying, she has thought on countless occasions since, how time, place and person came together, all wrapped up, as it were, in a neat parcel. But the string broke: the time did not last, the place was not hers, and the man never loved her.

I r e n e   Through the back window of this house which is not mine I see rain is falling steadily: the draped statue in the garden is glistening and the chairs have been propped against the table in the middle of the soaked lawn, a sign that summer is definitely over. Fat raindrops rest on the leaves of the fig tree, and suddenly I notice a small bunch of purple grapes hanging from the vine near the back door. A surprise, this: it was not actually clear to me until now that grapes could grow in England. The vine shelters slender white cyclamens growing, carefully tended, in pots, and immediately I see the miniature purple ones that are springing up all over the Peloponnese right now, in their own season of mellow sunlight.

I twist my bright yellow worry beads with their knotted and tangled tassel: a symbol of revolt against Vasili, this purchase, for women in Greece do not have, let alone use, worry beads. I twist them and finger them separately and think about light.

I used to take light, Greek light, Australian light, for granted until I came to London. I now find myself crossing the street in order to walk on the sunny side.

It came to me quite suddenly once that the Greek Αδής, Hades, means unseen. Hell is not fire but the absence of light, not being able to see or be seen, the plunge into utter blackness. I think of all those village widows wrapping their bodies in black, all those candles in church continually being snuffed out and replaced, Oedipus gouging his eyes out. Of Homer, blind because that is what happened to bards: they were blinded so that, deprived of the sense of sight, their other senses, their memory and imagination, would be sharpened. Unable to see pictures, they had to compose them and hold them fast by means of constant repetition.

Irene herself was wilfully blind for a long period, but she sees now that this was probably for the best and that everything happens in its own time. The scales shifted from her eyes on several occasions but she replaced them very firmly, until this was no longer possible and they fell off altogether. Although she could not see herself very clearly, and still cannot, she saw enough to know that she was lost in the limitless desert of other people's expectations.

I r e n e Joachim is far better at geography than I am but I wonder whether he has ever considered the importance of the fact that Greece is not an island, even though it has four thousand of them floating about. People tend to forget that Australia is an island, but this is a vital point: an island mentality stays with you forever. Islanders feel safe because they are cut off, not threatened by borders. Of course this is an illusory safety, but it's very easy to ignore this fact.

I cannot ignore the fact that Michael is a cadet in the Greek army. And Greece has four borders. I try not to think of them, or of the tensions and trouble-spots. I do think of Virginia Woolf, who was never a mother but was still able to imagine what mothers go through, knowing what lies ahead of their children: 'love and ambition and being wretched alone in dreary places'. It must be very easy to be wretched alone in an army.

Last autumn, on Michael's nineteenth birthday, I rode through Durham on the train. Durham in the autumn is a glory: leaves gold, yellow, red and brown were falling so slowly it seemed possible to count the turns they made in the air. Stands of copper beeches towered beside the cottages brightly cloaked in Virginia creeper, and the castle and the cathedral were simply *there* – great brooding presences.

Michael had been in the army for a week and I had not heard a word. A year later he is the only one who writes, sending me postcards of central and northern Greece, places I have never seen. 'Dear Mum, I should be studying, but I can't be bothered . . . ' Mr Cool.

Last year, on that day on the train, I tried to imagine what his army life would be like but failed completely, because at heart I did not want to know. All I could think about was his beautiful hair: when he was three he had a mop of autumn-gold curls. The thought of a half-inch stubble was almost more than I could endure. But of course I did endure it and now have seen him, often, in uniform, and looking like a convict out of it. I think of Juliet and Joanna and the sheer hell of raising daughters in rural Greece. But at least daughters do not have to do national service.

I worry that my selfishness, my determination to make my sons Australian Greeks, has made their lives difficult. Thomas certainly finds what he calls 'this two countries business' difficult. He has to choose soon. Michael has already done so, in his decision to join Greece's regular army, but he said, when he returned from Melbourne last summer, 'I don't know when I'll get there again now.' And he looked away from me and said nothing further.

Surely I am right in thinking that Joachim, the only Greek-born one, will find it easier? On holiday in Melbourne he and I used to make regular trips to the local fish-and-chip shop, owned by two Greek men long established in Australia. They asked Joachim the inevitable questions. 'Which do you like best, Greece or Australia?' Joachim was the soul of tact. He looked at them steadily and said, 'Australia's beautiful. Really good. But not forever.'

A r t e m i s   I open my eyes and see that somebody has put chrysanthemums, the • flowers of Saint Dimitrios, in a jar on the table. So it is autumn. The thought comes to me suddenly. Yes, it is autumn. And equally suddenly I think how I miss my garden. Not that I ever planted many flowers. Pretty things, but wasteful – space is always needed for aubergines, artichokes, lettuces, beans, tomatoes, onions and garlic, and other things besides. How I remember all that digging, planting, hoeing, weeding and hard work.

My foreign *nífi* was the one for flowers. Perhaps she has put these on the table. No, I do not think this can be so, for I would have heard if she had returned. But she was the one who brought me flowers. She would give me other presents as well. I would thank her and laugh. Often I threw them out or gave them away. What did I want with soaps and scents? I always used my own olive-oil soap for everything. Other presents, now I remember, were dull bowls and plates from the local potteries. Useless, old-fashioned stuff. I wanted bright plastic dishes, modern things instead, and told her so. She gave presents at Christmastime, which was wrong. Άγιος Βασίλης, the Feast Day of Saint Basil the Great, New Year's Day, is present-giving • day.

I focus on the flowers, mauve, yellow and pink, and then feel the thread of thought break. No, it doesn't break; it drifts free as the long piece of spider's web does when you walk into it. It is floating away from me but I lean forward, or my mind does, and I pluck at it gently, willing it to return. It moves back and forth, evading the finger of my mind. I stop trying because I feel so tired, and then, the disobedient thing, it comes back and joins up again.

And the thought is: I kept the crochet magazines she bought me. Yes, I did. Well, why not? I was bored with my own patterns, learned from my mother, handed down from my yiayia and practised for fifty years or more. It was a simple matter to look at the pictures and learn new patterns, new σκέδια. It took only one good look, usually, and perhaps a bit of counting. She, the foreign wife, always had to *read* the patterns, poring over the squiggled marks on the page. This was something I could never understand: she couldn't do anything without the help of books. My son once found a book about goats somewhere in his house. Goats! How we laughed over that when he told me. It was all useless, naturally. She didn't know anything about goats and couldn't learn, and I told her so. She still can't make cheese. I know that for a fact, and keep remembering it. Unless she's learned to make it where she is now. In England? I think that's where they told me she is. Do the English eat cheese? I do not know. It is not necessary to know such things.

She even tried to learn our language through books. Only a Greek can speak Greek, as is natural and right. Our language is so difficult, has so many words. Even I do not know them all, so what did she expect? So many words for rock, I remember. What use are books? She was a foolish, stubborn girl. She should have talked to me more; she should have sought my company. She was shy as well, would not speak up. She was a problem, a great problem.

Her papers and books were another. They were everywhere in that house. That was one good thing about the move, now I recall: the mess was no longer in *my* place. It was my habit to visit my son's house three times a day, and it didn't matter much what time it was, there she would be, either sitting scribbling or clacking away at the machine, the name of which I do not know, or wandering around with a book in her hand. My poor son. His poor sons. I would lift a pile of papers from a chair, sit down and tell her to keep on working. Of course it wasn't work at all, but what could I say? I would talk to her, do my best to entertain her, because I know mothers need company when their children are at school. I would ask her about the children's lunch, about what my son could expect when he got home from work, all those things. I did what mothers-in-law and *yiayiáthes* do.

Papers, books. What else? Something is nagging at me. What is it? Just wait, old woman. It will come. Ah yes, letters. She was always writing them, particularly to her mama. Well, that, I suppose, was right. But it

197

was shameful the way she used to haunt the post office. I do not like to think, even now, of the postmen and what they thought. Perhaps it is not so important, as they are not from here, those postmen, are not *ours*.

She kept herself very much to herself, the foreign *nifi*, but I have seen her face fall on mornings when there were no letters waiting for her. I do not know why letters were so important. Sometimes six, or even more, would come at once, and her eyes would crinkle around the edges as they always did when she smiled. Letters seemed to make her smile quite often.

At other times I would see her sitting and gazing and thinking the good God knows what. She thought too much, had too much time in which to think. Like me, now. I cannot say that I like these endless hours. Thinking is not a pleasure. And now it takes such effort it hardly seems worth it. But I have nothing else to do except feed myself. At least I can do that. And now that I am very old all I want to eat is meat. Before, meat was something I ate very occasionally, and at Christmas and at Easter. Everybody eats meat at Christmas and Easter.

Thinking. Ageing. Τα γεράματα, old age. I wonder if the foreigner has thought about old age yet. She should, for she is certainly not young any more. She should be thinking of doing real work, of looking to her property and to getting the big boys married to respectable rich girls of good family. That might be another problem: she might want her sons to marry foreigners. But it will be nothing to do with her, as it was nothing to do with me when my eldest son went away and came back married.

She much prefers to be with foreigners. Why? What do they know? What does she want with them? She is *ours*, and was ours as soon as she married, even if she didn't know it. She became ours in every way as soon as she came here to live.

She is ours and should be looking forward to her grandchildren, who will be our children. It matters little whether I am alive or not, or whether she is. They will still be ours, part of the pattern and fabric of family. What else does she want? What else could anybody want? I do not understand her at all.

My eyes are still fixed on the flowers. Who could have brought them? Joachim, perhaps. That is the sort of thing his mother encouraged. His mother: I have thought about her too much today. It does not do. The effort exhausts me and is useless, anyway, as all my efforts are now.

It is evening again. Another evening and the light is failing.

J u l i e t   My English friends have left at last. They think the sun makes up for everything but this is only because they are from the north. 'I'm here to tell you that there is more

to life than the weather,' I say tartly. And then they're
always glad to leave, to get back to London, to their
own places where they know the territory, where they
no longer need maps and compasses, where they fit,
where they can use a kind of shorthand in conversation and take for granted the comfort of familiarity.

The sun doesn't make up for grace, elegance, the
occasional touch of luxury, a certain softness – all
things which have never been part of Greek village
life. Pavlos understands this, or seems to, for we never
talk about it. Perhaps there isn't any need to, as we've
known each other so long; we never discuss the things
I miss. Occasionally we go out to dinner, but Joanna
will stay home. We don't discuss this either, but Pavlos
knows that I like us to dine out as a couple. That's
rather unusual, that flash of understanding – here,
where the family is so important, where everything is
supposed to be done for the good of the children, τα
παιδιά. The children.

I have two or three favourite places in the town.
It's still quite possible to eat outside, even in October,
and I like to sit and look at the sea and the lights glistening on the water. We don't talk much; perhaps we
don't need to. We talk about the food and try to
decide whether we'll have *calamária* or *moussaká* and
invariably end up having both. I drink too much,
because I like retsina and always have done, and
because it's the kind of wine that slips down easily and

then creeps up on you. And into your head. I relax, let go a little, and feel that there is a softness here after all: I think of warm evenings, the rose light, and of my beautiful Greek child. And then Pavlos says, because he likes to please me – well, most of the time he does – that if the olive harvest goes well we might be able to go to Santorini for a little while. In June, after school breaks up and before the crowds come. What do I think? You know what I think, I say, smiling at him. I've always wanted to go to Santorini. We'll see, he replies, pleased at my reaction. Santorini, or Rhodes or Samos.

I know perfectly well that we probably won't get to any of those places, but it doesn't matter. I understand Pavlos, I understand the Greek capacity for living in the moment, I understand the Greek attitude towards promises and intentions. It's taken a lot of work to reach this point but I've managed it.

We drive home, Pavlos and I, look in on Joanna, smile at each other and go to bed. Sometimes. Or sometimes he goes to see his mother, or his sister or his brother or his closest cousin, just to say goodnight, just to settle into the groove again, and I sit down to my diary, which he never asks me about.

I've settled into this world now; it's my place and I couldn't be happy in another. Irene always said it was too small for her. I know what she means, for it's too small for me too, in a way, but individuals have their own, very different ways of making a tiny world expand. Irene, poor thing, has that streak of creativity which so often leads to rebelliousness and restlessness. She sees endless possibilities, has a sense of the variety of life, of all sorts of combinations: she has curiosity and couldn't understand, not ever, the villagers' lack of it. There's a whole world out there that they know nothing about, she would moan. They don't want to know about it. I used to look at her and think, yes, well, you can't force knowledge on people, at least not without grim consequences. And this lot's secure in their ignorance, they've got their certainties and they're happier and more contented than you're ever going to be. She knew what I thought. She'd look at me and drop the subject.

She was deeply frustrated but she struggled on for a very long time. Her good manners made things even more difficult for her. Her reluctance to make scenes, her readiness to put up with a great deal without complaining didn't do her any good at all. She tried to cope alone. She had to; there wasn't any support available, except from me. Greek village women are expected to be self-reliant without being challenging or rebellious. The family Irene married into was used not only to self-reliant women but to tough ones. Take old Artemis, for example — not that anybody would want to. Now, there's a survivor. She's admirable and all that, you have to admit it, but hardly comfortable to live with.

A form of vicious circle starts with good manners, I think. The more you show good manners and appear to be coping alone, the more people think you are managing well and the more they leave you to your own devices, and so your loneliness increases. They don't seem to know anything here about the need for support, kindness, protection, just plain love. I've abandoned good manners. I don't cope alone, I don't even pretend to.

I *demand* Pavlos's support. I lose my temper whenever necessary. This is a calculated effort at getting what I want. Quite coolly and calmly, I fly into a rage. It's the only thing to do and the effort's not often wasted. Pavlos can't expect me to repeat the old ways of his mother's life. I told him so at the start, and Irene should have told her husband the same thing. I also know, and have always known, that I'll have to fight for Joanna and teach her lessons. There are at least three to be learned, I think. Men mustn't expect women to put up with everything; women have a responsibility to themselves; neither men nor women have the right to think that being a woman means being sacrificial.

The other thing Irene should have done was decide. She should have decided on one country or the other. She should have chosen. People do fall in love with foreign countries but Irene seems rather promiscuous in this respect. When it comes to people she is the most constant individual I know, doglike, almost, in her faithfulness and attachments, but she is easy in her affection for places. Joanna knows she's Greek but I'm not so sure about Joachim and his brothers. They slip and slide, apparently very easily, between countries, languages and cultures, but is it all as simple and as effortless as it appears? In cross-cultural marriages, partners often compete for the souls, minds and spirits of their children. This is not necessarily a conscious process but it does go on. I've seen it happen and so I wonder about Joachim and his brothers.

People have to choose, they have to settle, and this is precisely what Irene is not doing. She's past mid-life now, although an optimistic English friend of mine maintains that people these days are middle-aged until they're sixty. What does she hope for? How can she bear to live in other people's houses, on the edge of other people's lives in this way? She isn't part of anybody's life as far as I can gather. At our age we need somewhere to potter, our own place. She's got nowhere.

I know my place. I've earned the knowledge, and the right to property, to certainty. This is the way things should be at my age. At our age.

Irene, in gregarious mood on a soft fine day, joins a motley assembly of people who are intent on keeping the ancient custom of Beating the Bounds, to mark the borders of parishes on Hampstead Heath. Her thinking, as it is with so many other things, is divided about this. On the day, she is fascinated by the history of this practice and the fact that it has lasted. But she is also repelled by the long tentacles of custom. Yearning quite vainly to be free of the bondage and tyranny of the past, she finds herself thinking, Spare me this folksy stuff. Very early in the proceedings she takes her willow bough, used in the striking of the marker stones, and throws it away.

But she is deeply impressed by the fact that there are trees on the Heath that are six hundred years old, and makes a mental note to tell Joachim, even though she knows that he, living in the Ancient World and surrounded by olive trees, will not appreciate her reaction. She places the trees against an historical fact: she will point out to Joachim that these trees were planted before the Fall of Constantinople.

I r e n e   The sight of squirrels reminds me of Joachim and all his insects and animals, the way he used to spot glow-worms in the hedges, and come back from the river covered in mud and carrying a bucket half-full of tadpoles. When he was four he went hunting cicadas, found wasps instead and was badly stung. A full-scale tantrum followed.

'Wasps!' he yelled. 'Bloody bastards!' The Australian graft had started to take.

There was always a cat. Tigger was a tabby Joachim lugged about wherever he went; Pete was a pure white whose tabby tail and back legs made him look for all the world as if he were wearing a pair of grey flannel trousers. Then there was Red, whom we lost. And now there is Asprouli, 'the little white one', with tabby patches.

Old Maria gave Joachim Tigger when they were both very small, sending Joachim home with a minute scrap in a cardboard box. Vasili was not pleased. My mother was visiting the village then and dedicated hours to feeding the mewling bundle with an eye-dropper, so that Tig grew and prospered and developed into a harmless and necessary cat. Most mornings Vasili, leaving the house before everybody else, would find a dead field mouse, and sometimes only half a one, deposited neatly on the doormat. Once again he was not pleased.

One day Tig went walkabout and never returned; was he a Greek cat, after all? Shortly after his disappearance, Joachim and I rescued three kittens left to gasp their last in the middle of a clump of prickly pear. They were shockingly thin, but once again steady feeding with the eye-dropper wrought a miracle and all three soon resembled nothing so much as furry, perambulating cricket-balls. We gave the lot away.

By the time trouser-clad Pete came to stay my parents were back in the village.

'What are you going to call him?' my father asked Joachim.

'Pit,' he replied succinctly.

'Odd name for a cat.'

The mysteries of the Greek accent were solved eventually: Pit was actually Pete.

Joachim cannot imagine life without Toby, who is now in his eleventh year but has not slowed down at all. He's Michael's dog, in fact. Michael plagued Vasili for a puppy until Vasili, almost demented, gave his consent in a weak moment he has regretted ever since.

A short time later, in his first year at high school, Michael loved learning about Odysseus's dog, who recognised his master but was so old and enfeebled that he could only wag his tail in greeting. Toby communicates. He leans against people and demands to be cuddled; he loves the sound of English; he lifts sun-hats off heads; he remembers. He cried every time my parents walked up the garden path; they were away for two years at a stretch but it made no difference, and now he cries and whimpers when I come back. Even though everything has changed and can never be as it was, his bark has the comfort of familiarity, is part of the sound of home.

Teaching has always been part of Irene's life; she has carried on a family tradition established by her grandfather who fled a career as a publican. Irene's mother wanted to be an actress but was forced to be a teacher instead. She found she was, with her love of little children, a very good one, and so contrived to be happy in her work.

Irene was not so happy in hers. A sheltered child of the 1950s, she was never permitted to see the notorious film *Blackboard Jungle*, but consistently thought of the classroom as an essentially primal scene, with teacher as prey, pupils as stalking, skulking, scheming predators. When Hobbes was penning his immortal lines about the life of man being solitary, poor, nasty, brutish and short, he obviously had schoolteachers in mind. So Irene thinks.

I r e n e   At some stage when he was still quite small Joachim told me I ought to get a proper job. 'What do you mean, a proper job?' I asked.

'Well,' he replied, 'you need to get yourself an orange uniform and then you can be a check-out lady at a supermarket in Kalamata.'

It must have been about this time that I gave up teaching, said I'd never teach again. This was dangerous. Never say never. Saying never is like waving a red rag at the already rampaging bull of fate. I ought to know: I learned this lesson the hard way.

Retirement had been an ambition for years, but this time I thought it had happened, that I'd really succeeded in hanging up my chalk, so to speak. But teaching refused to give me up; once more I had chalk-dust in fingernails, hair and lungs, stacks of books to mark and lessons to prepare.

I had all sorts of reasons for wanting to give up teaching. I was becoming too old and crabby. Older and crabbier, my children said. I was still trying to teach my ingrates the rudiments of English and felt that this was enough; teaching one's offspring falls into the category of refined torture. Selfishness also reared its ugly head. Life is short and what was I doing with it, for Heaven's sake?

So I began, in my humble way, to emulate the example set by author Tom Sharpe: writing in the mornings, gardening in the afternoons, to which routine I added some Greek lessons and a few quiet sojourns into the surrounding countryside. But somebody – providence, fate, the furies – decided that that way fatness lies, considered that I was enjoying myself too much, that I was having my own way far more than was good for me. And so a deputation from the local community came to call.

With great enthusiasm this deputation explained a new development in Greek education: certain primary schools were to extend their curricula to include physical education, a foreign language, art, craft and music. Excellent, I remarked, trying to ignore the turn the conversation was taking. Physical education had already been established; next on the list was the foreign language requirement. Could I? Would I?

I dithered and slithered, feeling the steely bands of responsibility closing. The deputation did not depart. Only three hours a week. And you have taught the books. And, it added sorrowfully, nobody else will come. And even more sorrowfully, if we cannot have English classes we cannot go on to have art, craft and music. That did it: faced with the prospect of sleepless nights spent wrestling with my conscience, I gave in at once, albeit not gracefully. I was annoyed and resentful: discipline and effort would be called for and I would have to wear, among other things, a skirt, a wedding-ring, and a light application of spackle on the fading, pot-holed complexion.

In my first year of teaching, nearly thirty years ago, I taught thirty-seven periods out of a possible forty and spent much of my working life in a haze of fatigue. The school was visited regularly by a tyrannical district inspector who was ever on the look-out for the deadly sin of sloth. The only indications of a good conscientious day's teaching, he informed us, were an aching back and a raging headache. If we were free of these symptoms then we hadn't worked hard enough.

What with these formative experiences and my reloca-
tion to the land which taught the world about Tragedy
and its inevitability, I might have known that sooner or
later a return to teaching would be my lot.

And so to meet Grade 4. Vasili drove me to school
in the pouring rain.

'Are you cold?' he asked solicitously.

'No,' I grunted ungratefully.

'Then why are you shivering?'

I told him why.

'You're mad,' he said.

On arrival at the school he bundled me out of the
car and bellowed at the staff, half of whom he had
known for forty years.

'Look after the girl, won't you?' Standing grouped
on the balcony, the staff flashed winning smiles and
chorused the Greek equivalent of 'no worries'.

The headmaster, a man of courtly charm, escorted
me to the classroom and introduced me. With a sink-
ing heart I discovered that the class was his own and
that his son was in the class, as was the daughter of
another staff member. I still don't know what he
thought when, a few weeks later, he opened the classroom door and saw me on all fours saying energeti-
cally, 'Woof, woof. What am I?'

The other thing that made my heart sink was the
smallness of this world, of which relatives' expectations were such an important part. Some of Joachim's

second, third and fourth cousins were in that class, and some children had already started attending a *frontistirio* or language school, while a couple of others had relatives in the States, so that I was soon being told that I didn't teach like 'my other teacher', and that in the States *o kosmos* said 'zee' instead of 'zed'. Then there was the problem of not being attuned to the age group, and the quite unimaginable one of what it is like controlling a class while using a second language. When you are simulating anger or outrage in a classroom ('Panayioti, how *dare* you throw your rubber around in that fashion? Start work immediately!') you shouldn't have to worry about your grammar.

The inspector called: Errol Flynn moustache, carefully draped overcoat, beaming smile, the lot. He all but slapped me on the back, and I had the impression that he considered me a twenty-year-old who had never set foot in a classroom before. 'Here,' he said, thrusting a wad of notes at me. 'Read these, follow the instructions, and you'll be the perfect teacher in no time.' I felt duty-bound to remark that such a creature does not exist. Not at all daunted he said, 'Just do your best!' and sailed off, not having breathed a word about aching backs.

But the really amazing thing was that Yiayia was thrilled. She considered that I had arrived, in a sense, after quite a few years of travelling. It didn't matter to her that this was a lowly little job with truly abysmal pay. No, I had achieved status on her home territory and that was the main thing. She also loved hearing vignettes of life as lived by the nine-year-old set.

The job only lasted a year. The shepherd's wife, whose daughter had been in my class, said to me when it became obvious that I was not going to be re-employed, 'So they gave you the sack, eh? Bad luck. Evgenia says you were quite good.'

At home with me, when he was a little boy and his brothers were at school, Joachim spoke English. But when he built roads and cities in the garden, scrabbling around in the dirt with broken bricks and bits of wood, or constructed shops out of blocks on the kitchen floor, he spoke Greek, talking to himself, pretending to be various other people.

One language feeds the other. Thomas was very pleased when June taught him the word enigmatic. 'The Mona Lisa has an enigmatic smile,' she said, but now it is impossible to remember whether Thomas already knew the Greek αίνιγμα, the enigma, or not. And one culture feeds another. Once, when Thomas was at kindergarten in Melbourne, he asked the other children about their parents' voting patterns. 'My father votes Liberal and my mother votes Labor. My mother loves Gough Whitlam and my father hates him,' he announced matter-of-factly, to the great interest of the teacher. 'I've never had children discuss politics before,' she remarked to me, tactfully ignoring that early evidence of schism in the household. 'He's got a Greek father,' I reminded her.

When Thomas was much older he recounted a conversation he had had with some girls at the university where he was studying. 'My mother,' he informed them, 'is the worst mother in Greece.' Of course they wanted to know why. 'Well,' he intoned, 'she refuses to cook twice a day.'

回回

The last time they were in Melbourne together, Irene dragged Joachim everywhere: St Paul's Cathedral, which Irene once thought was quite large; Flinders Street Station; Southgate, which was as new to her as it was to Joachim, and a great improvement on the dingy river scenes of yesteryear. Spire and Concert Hall, Shrine of Remembrance and floral clock, they looked at them all. In the National Gallery, Joachim was struck by the McCubbin triptych *The Pioneers*, that archetypal rendering of early Australia, with hope defeated by the impersonal, merciless bush. What Irene took for granted was new to Joachim, so they had a history lesson right there and then.

And he was sympathetic when Irene reeled out of the gallery shop having been greatly shocked to find that a book she wanted was available only in Japanese.

'Whatever happened to English? We are in Melbourne, aren't we?' she asked, more than once.

It came to Irene then, that her Melbourne exists only as the city of her mind. The real place is situated on the road she did not take.

I r e n e   Death is the greatest change of all. Yellow leaves are drifting along Belsize Avenue in the light of a soft, pale sun and there is not a cloud in the sky. For once. I am remembering that Joachim was not in Melbourne when my mother died. I did not want him to be; I wanted him to remember her as she was at her golden wedding celebrations, as she was, still smiling, when she waved us both goodbye at Tullamarine.

I took Joachim back to the village and then returned to London, trying not to think about my next visit to Melbourne and the inevitability of it. I remembered looking at my mother during her last visit to Greece as she dozed in a chair in the spring sunshine. She felt warmed by it but I felt chilled: she looked very old. She was probably already ill and somehow I knew she would never visit the village again.

The summons came sooner, much sooner, than I had expected, and I went rushing back to the place I once called home and can never call home again. Of course the echoes of childhood were clamouring: they had been clamouring for some time. I want to write to Joachim about his grandmother so that he will remember her.

Mum was wife and mother to the last. 'Come on, chin up, get a grip on yourself,' she ordered briskly as I staggered, jetlagged and shaken with grief, toward her hospital bed.

'Yes, Mum,' I said obediently, even as I clutched her, and said it again as she reeled off a list of boarder/grandson Thomas's likes and dislikes. Four days later I received a phone call from my sister. 'Mum says there's a vitamin mixture on the second shelf in the pantry and you're to take it whatever you do.'

She agitated about the running of the house, even then. 'Do you want me to write everything down for you?' she asked. At that stage she could hardly stay awake, let alone hold a pen.

I was quite old, eighteen or twenty, before I realised, despite having read *Anna Karenina*, that unhappy marriages existed. How much I have learned and not learned since then. My parents knew each other for fifty-three years and joked with each other for most of them. I watched them continue to do so in my mother's hospital ward, grinning at each other in perfect understanding, happy for those moments. Often I turned away, overcome by their gallantry.

The last lucid remark Mum made to me will stay in my mind forever. 'He's a funny man at times,' she said, in certain knowledge and complete acceptance.

There was a day of great confusion during which she quoted lines about the bright and happy future, which once more made me turn away, sick at heart. She also tried, continually, to ring the airport.

'I can't get through,' she kept saying worriedly. I tried to tell her that there was no longer any need to do so. But ringing the airport had been part of her life, as Joachim and I came and went, as Thomas and Michael did likewise: much of our lives had been measured out in arrival and departure lounges.

When all hope had gone I wanted my mother to die on Australia Day, the 26th of January. In the event, she held on for another day. She was born in Albury, New South Wales, my mother – the foreigner, we called her – but she had spent most of her life in Melbourne, and there she died in her favourite season, with flowering gums and the purple blossoms of jacaranda just visible from the hospital window. She received the most marvellous care; the doctors and nurses assured us she was comfortable, but as I watched her struggle I couldn't see how that could possibly be true. She felt, I know it, what I have felt so often: she didn't want to stay but she didn't want to go either. And as I looked at her the terror of my own death was almost overwhelming. There is no such thing as a natural death, wrote Simone de Beauvoir: how right she was.

I am almost ashamed to tell Joachim that I wrote about his grandmother's death before, during and after it. Almost ashamed, but not quite, for we all have the right to keep functioning as best we can. My mother too wrote when things were at their toughest. I composed Greek death notices from us all, I scrubbed floors, I wrote and wrote. I woke up every morning and wondered what was wrong. And then I remembered: my mother was dead. Now that this had happened I was not a baby any more, even though this was what I most longed to be. I had been forced, finally, to grow up, even though I felt helpless, and cried, and wanted, above all, to be petted and comforted. Underneath are the everlasting arms, I was taught during long years of a nonconformist childhood, but now the arms I most wanted to be everlasting were gone forever.

When the phone call came I had been dusting her dressing-table, where a fading rose had dropped rusted petals. Twenty-four hours later the duster was precisely where I had left it and I still do not know why that seems odd.

I had a sense of disbelief: she had slipped out to the shops, was off on a brief holiday. But she never went on holiday without my father. My disbelief was balanced by necessity: her things had to be gone through. In the interim, I was poleaxed by discoveries: a hairpin in a corner of the lounge, the sight of the unfinished tapestry on the frame my father had made – it was a Greek scene; who would complete it now? The pseudo-Victorian statuette, ugly damn thing, that I bought for Mother's Day, 1958. I was almost thirteen, as Joachim is now. Nobody but a mother would have kept it, but there it was, with its card still attached, the handwriting just recognisable as mine: 'To Mum with Love'.

Learning to live without a person one loves is the hardest lesson of all. And we never stop learning, it seems.

The day after Mum's death, my brother and I were in a shopping centre.

'Strange how the world keeps going,' I remarked.

'It's reassuring, I suppose,' he replied.

No, it's not. It's a bloody cheek, I thought. But I said nothing, for he was right and I was wrong.

The thing about grief is that everybody else's is general and familiar; your own is unique and strange. After my mother's death I did not feel as I thought I would feel. I was worried and guilty because of my numbness. But perhaps I could feel no more because grief over absence, loss and separation had been part of my life for what seemed like forever. I did not know why there was so little pain but knew that I would welcome it as an active replacement for that dreadful weariness and dreariness, the sheer dullness of the house without her – in spite of the efforts we were all making.

I was locked in a limbo of inertia, suspended animation, but I kept functioning, kept busy somehow. Time slowed to the point where I thought I was moving through water or sand, but the days drifted by nonetheless. We slipped into a routine, my father and I, a routine pierced by moments like the one when my sister said, 'Mum was the only person who never disappointed me.' We got up, and we said things like, 'Today is the day we clean out the pantry. Tomorrow we might look at the linen press or the medicine cabinet.' In fact, however, we did not think about tomorrow if we could help it. We went to the shops, we ate too much or too little. We did not discuss it, but we were all thinking, What now? What is the point of anything, anyway?

The minister came and was wise, supportive, understanding. He had been through worse. He talked about the release from suffering. Coward that I am, I did not confess my resentment, my longing to ask the eternal questions: why did she have to suffer in the first place? Why must we suffer? Why must we die?

I used to tease my mother, as my children tease me. 'Songs and poems for all occasions,' I said. 'You'll be propped up in the old people's home, singing and reciting.'

'Better than crying,' she retorted once. She never made it to the old people's home, a fact I now resent but one she would be thankful for.

The funeral was moving and unmelodramatic. But I was undone by the tune of 'What A Friend We Have In Jesus'. That old thing; I'd forgotten all about it. The occasion was for me, at least, a mixture of tears and laughter, for, as the minister solemnly intoned, 'Ashes to ashes, dust to dust,' I swear I heard that certain and irrepressible laugh and that familiar voice saying, 'And if God doesn't get you, the Devil must!'

Back in Hampstead I went with Catholic friends to Mass at St Mary's, where I was struck down by the tune of Hymn 309 in the Presbyterian Hymnary: 'By Cool Siloam's Shady Rill'. What business that melody had in the middle of a Catholic Mass I have no idea, but I sat and cried like a baby, for I had sung it so many times standing beside my mother and knew that I never would again.

A r t e m i ş Joachim is here again, so it must be late afternoon. A whisper of memory tells me that he has always visited me at this time, before the next part of his day starts. He will go to play football or to practise his dancing. Once I was taken up to the *plateia* to watch him. There he was my little Ιωακείμ, wearing his great-grandfather's fustanella, all nine metres of pleats, and leading a row of docile little girls. People were very admiring. Well, so they should have been. Beautiful dancing is in his blood.

At this moment Joachim is sitting on the floor and playing with a kitten. A tiny scrap of a thing it is, and there are bits of screwed-up newspaper and twine all over my rug. You are failing indeed, old woman, if you let this happen in your kitchen. Once upon a time, παλιά, the child would not have dared do this. I'm not like his mother, the foreigner, who let that great monster of a dog into her *sala* every time there was bad weather.

But now I sit and think and say nothing. How important is it really, the state of my kitchen? The child's happiness is the only important thing; I wish his selfish mother agreed with me. He seems to be happy at this moment. He laughs his gurgling laugh every time the kitten takes a tiny swipe at the ball of newspaper, and laughs again at the various charges the little creature makes. I must say it is quite pretty: all fluffy and grey. But Joachim already has a cat. His father must be failing slightly, too, to allow another one in the house.

Children. Myself as a child. And now I cannot think of anything. I hate these times. A black cloud, a curtain, a blanket – something – settles on my brain and on my body. I don't know what it is. I haven't got the words to describe it or explain it. During these periods I sit – I have no idea how long I sit – until the cloud lifts and something snaps in my head and I am able once more to snatch at a thought as it flutters by. Like threads, like moths, like flames dancing on the hearth: thoughts are like all these things.

Children. They are different these days: that is the thought that went wandering. I think of myself when young. Not just young, small, when I was μικρούλα. No school for me, or very little. By the time I was eight I was doing most of the work I would continue to do for the next seventy years: the olive harvest, the fig harvest, weeding the vegetable garden, learning to cook, weave, crochet and sew. Learning to make cheese and soap and how to make use of every part of a pig. Not to mention how to kill chickens and rabbits. I could never kill kids – a weakness, that, I confess it. I confess to growing fond of them, although this weakness didn't stop me eating them at Pascha. This is our Easter custom, after all.

Work is not something that today's children concern themselves with over-much. Life is easy for them: school and games and dancing and new fashions and television and going out and spending, God protect us, a great deal of money. Parents are still working quite hard, it seems. Although not as hard as I used to.

My own children, who are all parents, are steady workers, doing all that is expected of them. Now I add to their burdens. I never wanted that. I do not want that now, but sometimes we have no choice in these matters. The foreigner's mother was never a burden to her. Not to anybody, I gather, or at least not for very long. A victory for her, a defeat for me. But I cannot complain, I have not had many defeats. I have done what I had to do: I have done what I set out to do. I have followed the pattern, the σκέδιο.

Most of my defeats have come about because of death. My parents, my brothers, my sisters, my husband and his brothers and sisters are all dead. I am the last of my generation. Well, somebody has to be, I suppose. And now I pray to our All-Holy One, Η Παναγία, for two blessings. I beg her, when I can concentrate and remember, to guard my children from every evil. Do not let my children die before their appointed time, I beg. I have already lost three. Δόξα το Θεό, Glory to God, I have seven left. Of course I pray for all the family, but a woman's children are always the most important. A child is part of a mother's body and, despite the awful wrenching and sundering, birth is a separation which is never quite completed. My children are bound to me with silken cords which have never broken. Men do not understand these things, which is why, very occasionally, a man may leave his family. Women, never. Greek women, that is. Village women who know what is natural and right. My foreign *nífi* has broken a sacred law. Αναθεμά την. Curse her. No pain, no sorrow could be too bad for her, no well of loneliness too deep.

I could wish her death, even pray for it, and not see my wishes and prayers as sin. She deserves to be punished. God will punish her, I am sure of that. God and the Evil Eye between them. But my little Joachim, να

224

μην αβασκαθή, may he not be envied, would be very unhappy if she died, as my children will be unhappy when I die. It would be too early for him, not the right time at all.

My thoughts flap and flutter. Sometimes they seem to rise and fall with my breath and then settle just out of reach. Questions. Answers. What is my other request of the *Panagía*? Ένας καλός θάνατος. That's it, a good death. No pain, or if that is asking too much, only a little – every woman's hope during childbirth. «Καλή ελευθερία», we say to women about to deliver. 'Good freedom.' We could make the same wish about death. Good freedom.

Now I am thinking clearly, but for how long? I wonder what death is like? I wonder if the foreigner's mother wondered? We remember nothing of our birth, so perhaps we remember nothing of our death either. That would be easy. I fear living too long, but it comes to me now that I also fear fear. Yes, I do. I do not want to be afraid at the moment of my death, as I would be if I were about to plunge into a well or enter a dark cave full of bats and other nameless horrors.

Charos, the ferryman, the Styx and Cerberus: how do I feel about this form of το τελευταίο ταξίδι, the final journey? I do not know and have not had the time or inclination to think about these things before. Why not think of light instead? Our Greek light: why should it not continue wherever we are? Light must be part of Paradise. Paradise must be sunny and warm, it must be. The *Panagía* knows that another part of this good death I so long for is a promise: the promise that I will meet my family and friends, my lost children once again. When I think of this promise I do not feel afraid of cold earth, or the wooden box in the charnel-house. My husband, the priest, used to tell me about this promise: he believed in it. And I of course believed in him.

J u l i e t   I did my Christian duty today and went to see old Artemis. I see Joachim almost every day, but every so often I tell myself that I ought to go and visit his yiayia. Not that I enjoy it, I never did. She was a combative, domineering woman, and although everything's changed and she's a shadow of her former self I can't forget the way things were. She had to be cock of her own dunghill – nothing surer than that – and of her great tribe of children. Joachim's father was her particular favourite, and putty in her hands. Favourite. Victim. She said jump and he would ask how high.

Of course matters were made worse by Irene's jealousy. She admitted, at least to me, that she's not good at sharing. It seemed to her that her husband always preferred other company, and preferred to upset her rather than upset anybody else. She wasn't far wrong, actually. She certainly never had the support she deserved and needed. Being the mother of three sons can't be easy, and she found it very hard work, particularly as she was quite determined that they, these half-Greek boys, should show some consideration for women. She had middle-class ideas about manners and rosters and washing-up and tidying rooms; she told them she was not a maid or a slave. She tried to insist on conversation at the dinner-table. Conversation on topics other than football and politics. Her ideas took, at least to some extent, but she used to complain to me that she was struggling alone. Perhaps she should have let those things drop.

Now everything's changed. Irene's gone and old Artemis sits all day, eyes closed, in her chair. At night they lift her into bed and in the morning they lift her out into the chair again. What a life, and it's dragged on like this for so long. Sometimes she knows her family but more often she doesn't. She smiles her toothless smile at Joachim, they tell me, whenever he's there, but apart from that nobody can guess at what goes on inside that head of hers, so close to being a mere skull.

We shook hands and I noticed she still has a very firm grip. The courtesies, like learned formulae, are still there. She asked the usual questions, but I'm sure my answers meant nothing to her and that she didn't have a clue who I was, even though I've been in that kitchen often enough and she knew me as Joachim's mother's friend.

That visit has got me thinking about time – past, present and future – and the only certainty there is, which is death. It's all too easy to think that the past *is* the past, done with, gone forever. As a teacher I've had to spend a lot of time thinking about the past continuous tense because it doesn't correspond exactly in Greek and English. In psychology, or memory, or lost love, or history, the past continuous is a problem because it expresses the past, which ought to be over, and the continuous, which obviously keeps on going. I've wondered about Irene and the past continuous many times. Australia, for example, represented her past life but it continued in her head, and she couldn't do anything about this constant renewal even though it hurt her. And now I wonder about England and whether something, somebody, some episode there, has affected her in the same way. I don't suppose I'll ever know.

There's nothing like the thought, or the vision, of imminent death to get you thinking about how much time you've got left yourself. We all know we're going to die but we never really believe it. This body, so familiar, so *mine*, will be here forever. So we think, in spite of all the evidence. Perhaps we think differently in our old age.

Old Artemis is so close to death as makes no difference. Well, perhaps it makes a difference to her. What if Joanna should die before I do? I would go mad if this happened: *my* death is the only separation from Joanna I can contemplate. I've not experienced the death of a parent yet. Mine are still relatively hale and hearty and manage to get themselves to Gatwick and over here at least once a year. Usually at Easter, because they love the wildflowers; sometimes they come during the summer and have a right old time complaining about the heat and all the things that annoy them about Greece and Greeks. 'Wouldn't you think,' says my father on seeing the men sitting at the *kafeneion* at eleven o'clock in the morning, worry beads twisting through their fingers, ouzo glasses and coffee cups at the ready, 'that they'd be out working?' I laugh but have learned not to say anything. Perhaps the old see the world as a foreign land. Perhaps old age, just as much as migration, is a form of exile, exile from our essential selves. The old, let's face it, have a different way of doing things.

I've an idea that at some stage Irene recognised her self, the self that she had had to disown so long ago, the English-speaking, rather bookish, curious self, in someone else, somewhere else. I don't know. But usually love says, 'You are myself,' and that projection, the recognition of a soul-mate, whatever it's called, can have drastic effects, especially in middle-age when we are all floundering about asking, Is this all there is?

My mother isn't as old as Kyra Artemis but it won't be long before she's eighty. Now that I think about it, her basic expectations were much the same as Artemis's: work, the raising of a family, time to see and enjoy her grandchildren. Her marriage, a young marriage, wasn't arranged, although the British upper classes rather favour arranged marriages even now. You can see the result, the boredom, in those patrician faces. My mother is a romantic. She fell in love with my father and is still in love with him. He thinks he loves her, she thinks he loves her, and so they contrive to be happy. But unlike Artemis she wanted a range of rewards: companionship, emotional support, fun and adventure. She deserves more of these last than she's actually received, but has appreciated everything, really, has remained open to the new, the different, the unexpected, and change in general.

Is Artemis afraid of death? Death's never discussed here in Greece, although Greeks, fatalistic and secretive as they are, are very good at mourning, at coping with grief. They've a deep understanding of the psychology of it. And here in the village you mustn't ever mention cancer. I was warned not to: there must be some superstition connected with naming it, but I've never inquired.

Irene's mother died of cancer and was frightened. Irene told me that. 'I hated to think of her being afraid,' she said. 'She was never frightened of anything, or never appeared to be. And she didn't tell me she was frightened. She told my father and then the subject of fear was never raised again. I couldn't have helped her,

Juliet, because I'm frightened too. Of everything, really, life as well as death. I'm just not brave. We're so different, you and I.'

I miss Irene very much. I miss her conversation, the fact that she was always there. I miss her.

I r e n e   I seem to have a great many sleepless nights. I hate them. They are always crammed with thoughts of Joachim, his collections. His jam jars and boxes full of shells gathered over summers, the rows of empty cartridge cases, the lumps of quartz gleaming and endlessly faceted that we found behind the village. His two snow scenes in bubbles: one of Father Christmas and reindeer, and one of Melbourne, where snow never falls, showing the Arts Centre and a St Kilda Road tram. Glorious in their kitsch. The Greek coins, the little earthenware wombat, the luminous yo-yo and a small box full of incense, no doubt pinched from church during his altar-boy phase. I can picture every item in his room.

Being a Greek boy, Joachim never had a doll. But I bought Thomas one when he was small and we were living in Melbourne. I thought Vasili would expire with mortification and after that I didn't buy any more dolls. I didn't like to tell Vasili that the dolls' corner was a favourite place of Thomas's at kindergarten.

Tomorrow I must make a list of birthday presents.

Licorice all-sorts are mandatory, as are tapes by various bands beyond my ken, as well as an extremely complicated Lego set. I already have a list of possible model numbers.

I have no idea how Joachim will react to these letters I have not yet sent, but perhaps he realises that letters from loved people are something to have and to keep, proper presents, ones that last. I, for example, have a small bundle of quite ordinary letters, not even hand-written, which I don't imagine I will ever burn. Joachim can always put my letters away to read later. Perhaps he will understand then; perhaps the letters will be an explanation as well as a present.

He must want some sort of explanation. Surely everybody does? Myself, I'm like Dostoevsky: I want to be there, wherever 'there' is, when everything is explained clearly so that I know what it's all been about. The tugs of love, for example, and the absences. And the nature, so elusive, of happiness.

His yiayia, when she was beginning her slow decline into that twilight world of senility, pinned me with a sharp look on one occasion and asked abruptly, 'Are you happy here?' I started; over the years I had believed that the thought of my happiness never entered her head, that indeed she never thought of happiness at all. One does what is expected in a peasant life and derives satisfaction from it. Happiness is another matter.

I looked at Artemis warily and said, 'I've got used to

it.' Happiness was another matter to me too by then.

She smiled thinly and remarked, with a flash of the old confidence, 'You'll get *more* used to it.' I could tell she was already drifting away from me, from this slight conversation, from reality. At times she would return, but now she stays away, is not part of what we call the real world at all.

I didn't, of course, get any more used to it. I must point out to Joachim that I am not the only one who considers migration a form of suicide, a journey through pain. The death of the old self is necessary, and part of the pain is the slow accumulation of knowledge: of the new culture, most often acquired with great difficulty, and also the knowledge, which comes sooner or later, that an advance in understanding is impossible. This recognition of impossibility, which may come in a flash or creep up stealthily, was followed in my case by a depth of fatigue which I hope Joachim never experiences. Other migrants have written about this: a migrant I once read about used simply to faint quite regularly because of it. I developed insomnia.

Part of the problem was that I simply did not understand the ancient world. Europeans think that Australia has no history; Australians think that Europe has too much. I did not understand, even though I had read about them, the layers of race-memories, the deep conflicts, the lasting hatreds, the festering feuds, that sense of rankling injustice which is so much part of Greek history. All this, I thought, was nothing to do with me. What arrogance, what heedlessness. One thing I did understand was the instinct to survive, that grim power to endure, because it is part of me too, even though the peasant acceptance, the fatalism, the *habit*, were all beyond me. Incomprehensible. Uncertainties are simply not permitted in rural Greece and this meant that I, uncertain creature that I am, was not permitted to be myself.

The sooner Joachim learns that uncertainty is part of life the better. I think he is already learning this through me, and my uncertain presence. The pioneers knew all about uncertainty and accepted it. They were better prepared for disaster than the average old-world peasant. They also took risks; the average peasant doesn't. I've taken risks because I have had to. The alternatives, stagnation, decay, death, were far worse to contemplate than a gamble. Then too, change takes place anyway, despite all our efforts and pretence.

People, with the exception of Juliet, have always accused me of painting a negative picture of Greece. I would, if I could, paint an entirely black picture of it. I would, if I could, turn my back on the place which has so wounded me, for my life would be much simpler that way. But I cannot do it. Even if I did not have – and what a truly appalling thought this is – Joachim and his brothers, I could not do it. Greece has almost broken me but it is part of me nevertheless. It has a grave enchantment that was almost my undoing. Those who talk about the light-hearted Mediterranean are completely wrong, for those shores are weighted with sorrow and soaked in blood. Landscape is not merely geography and topography, it is history and emotion as well. I was willing to be enchanted by Greece because of Vasili and his blind, devoted attachment to it. And now I am attached to Greece – its landscape, whatever it is that makes it what it is – for its own sake and for mine.

There is, in the Greek landscape, an almost immediate attraction for Australians – it has that bareness, that starkness we are so accustomed to. It is not like the green embroidered over-stitchedness of much of the rest of Europe. The intensity works a potent magic. The harshness of the rock, the glare of the light. That skinned, peeled sea.

And in some strange interaction of environment and personality, every Greek seems to have an anarchic streak which I applaud and envy, as I applaud and envy the vitality of their nature, the ability to live in the present moment while bearing the burden of the past. And the quicksilver quality of personality – which is not the same as attitude to life – that light and shade, the interchanging of the comic and the tragic masks. But how to explain the secretiveness, the deviousness in all that glare? A long history of wars and occupations, perhaps, which would also explain the tendency to fatalism and melancholy.

Name-days being of the great significance that they are in Greek culture, I have always felt Joachim slightly hardly done by, for Saints Thomas and Michael are more important than Saint Joachim. But a thirteenth birthday is significant: he is about to start the long haul to manhood. I shall tell him not to worry, for he will get there and will be able to use the word happiness very frequently, because of the way he is. He gives it, quite naturally, without thinking about it. People, especially me, have only to be near him to be happy. A rare gift. Foreign visitors, whose guide and interpreter he is, remark on this, and on how he knows everybody and everybody knows him.

Joachim and I are happy, in the simplest possible way, when we are together, and he is part of nearly every bright moment that I remember in the village. But it was never just a matter of him and me. There were the complications of other people, the place itself and my spirit. Many attempts were made to break my spirit, and then it started to dwindle anyway through despair and loneliness. When I was with Joachim I was all right, but I was often bad for him. Finally it was time to go. If I have a lesson to teach him it is this: don't let anybody break your spirit. Not ever.

Joachim may know, even now, something of the mysterious nature of love. Anyone can love anyone, I believe. The heart has its reasons, which I long to understand, and its favourites, and a will of its own. Once, my heart became unexpectedly wilful and way-ward, and I felt awake, real, *seen*. It was so easy to be happy then. I was not in Greece but I felt twice as alive, bathed in a gentle, soft light. The softness was what I wanted, and still want, after all those shrivelling rays.

It comes down to this: Greece very nearly defeated me, it demanded an unconditional surrender which I could not give. But I would not have missed those bat-tles and skirmishes over rough and rugged terrain for anything. And I'm still alive, even if being alive involves a great deal of living in my head and holding conversations with absent people.

Conversation in Greece was always a problem. There were no reassuring certainties, no echo at all, and there never can be an echo, in my opinion, from a language that is not your first. There was only the feel-ing that I unsettled people when I tried to converse. But I was, and am, the unsettled one.

Morning at last; it is a grey one. I set out for the post office. As usual. It is a grey day. In the weeks that I have been sorting old letters and writing notes the leaves on the lime trees in the street have turned deep yellow and are starting to fall, faster and faster. Soon there will be none left.

In the Hampstead post office people are queuing

quietly, the light is pale. Outside, the traffic moves slowly. Back where Joachim is, in the village, the bus will be squeezing round that tight corner near the police station, gouging out a lump of balcony concrete on its way, as it has done before. Petros will be roaring cheerfully while sorting the mail, and Aristides will be moving slowly in response to the demands of a peasant who wants to post a letter to America. Petros will almost certainly bring Joachim something from me, a message by card or letter, for such messages make my world expand and bring him momentarily closer. But love is stronger than separation and so he is never far away. And I'll come if I can. When I can – I'll see him soon.

I stand in the queue in the Hampstead post office and although it is not nearly time yet I say, Happy Birthday, Joachim.

A r t e m i s It is back again, that buzz in the conversation that swirls around me. How else can I describe it – that change of feeling in this small kitchen which means that she, the foreign wife, has returned. I can never quite decide about the nature, the quality of this change. Of course Joachim is happy. As for the others, are they? Or are they indignant? Accusing? I do not think they know what they feel. They are wary, my children, waiting to see what will happen, whether she will stay, and for how long, or whether she will leave again. They do not know what to do and so they just wait and watch. As I do. But I have no choice in the matter – they have. Even though I do not know how long she will stay, I knew she would come back again. That is the way mothers are and have to be.

I want something. A moment ago I was quite certain what it was but now I have forgotten. Sit and wait. Just wait, it will come. And there, suddenly, it is: I want to go to church. I know this is impossible but I long to go again, just once more. The priest comes and I suppose he gives me communion, although I can never remember anything about it. I don't like him, anyway, and never have, even though we grew up together. But I am past worrying about having such a feeling about a man of God. The trouble is that he isn't a man of God and never was. My husband was – but he was too soft, too saintly, as was Papayianni. He's dead, too. But this one, he puts himself first and always has done, and is not kind: he beats his wife still. His mother was a witch. I'd forgotten that until just now, and γυναίκες, the women, used to say that he knew spells and magic and was not above dabbling in both. It is a pity I cannot ask him whether he has anything for errant wives.

A cracked laugh: I realise all at once that it is mine. They turn and stare at me; it is so long since any of us has heard this sound. Well, I can't say that I find life at all amusing but the thought of the foreign *nífi* being under a spell is. But then she has been under a spell, an evil one, for quite a long time.

I want to go to church and light candles to the *Panagía* – Παναγία, All-Holy Virgin, Blameless Lady, Mother of God. I want to beseech her to use her power for Joachim's sake and for ours: make the *nífi* stay, I want to plead. Make her stay. The saints would still be staring unwinkingly from the iconostasis, as they always have: Saints Theodore, Gregory, George, John Chrysostom, Elijah and Peter clutching the keys to Heaven. I seem to remember them all very well, but it is to the Mother of the Lamb that I wish to speak. She would bend her sorrowful gaze on me, as she used to, and I would open my old heart. But it will not happen. I cannot be taken to church now and it does not seem to occur to anybody that I might want to go. It is all they can do to get me out into my courtyard sometimes. When this happens I sit and watch the leaves drift: one by one now, there are so few left. These bright days will not last much longer.

No, I cannot go to church. A pity. I was always happy on Sundays. I had my own place and could sit comfortably through the whole three hours of the λειτουργία if I felt like it. My hand would be kissed a great many times simply because I am a παπαδιά, wife of a priest. It was a consolation. And now, after all that time, the thought comes creeping upon me: what do you do when such a consolation is not yours and never can be? The answer is, as it is so often, I do not know. What I do know is that it is very difficult to be happy. Happiness. I have not thought about it much. Such thoughts δεν κάνει, are not done, do not do.

Once, I cannot say when, I asked the *nífi* if she were happy here. It is not clear to me now why I asked. Perhaps I had already seen signs of trouble and was worried. I cannot remember. I do remember that she didn't say anything. Not at first. Her dark eyes turned to mine and she knitted her brows, as was her habit. Hers, lined as it is, is not a calm, relaxed face; it seems to me now that she has not known much peace. It is strange, that, when her very name means peace. A good Greek name. She would have known peace if she had only done what is natural and right and had continued to weave the set pattern, the οκέδιο.

Our eyes locked. I suppose that's one way of putting it. There was a long pause. And then she said something. What was it? Just wait. Ah yes. *Nai.* 'I've got used to it,' she said. «Το έχω συνηθήσει.» And what did I say? 'You'll get more used to it.' Yes, that is what I said, and what I hoped as I said it and for a long time afterwards. She didn't know it but my right hand, safely in my apron pocket, made the Sign of the Cross. I should have been braver and not hidden my hand. For look what happened anyway, in spite of all my efforts.

241

It has to be admitted that she too made efforts. As the years passed we came to understand each other a little better. The first time she came back my children, who do not always show me proper respect and continue to tease me with the mirror, asked me who she was. Sometimes I do not know what they want. I looked at her carefully and said, 'She's a Greek from Alexandria.' It was her accent; I couldn't place it, but with all her faults she speaks Greek correctly and looks rather like us.

She laughed when I said that and then I knew her, for she held her face close to mine and I saw her eyes crinkle around the edges as they always did when she smiled or laughed. In the old days she smiled and laughed quite a lot. She would crack a joke in her Greek with its odd accent and I would grin. Well, she *was* funny, and could make us all grin very readily. My smile would please her and her effort would please me.

The day I said she was a Greek from Alexandria she said, 'Thank you for the compliment, Yiayia,' and time slid away from me then, for she was always polite, it has to be said. But now, what has it all come to? And what will become of us all?

J u l i e t   Irene didn't let me know she was coming but I'm not hurt – I've an idea that she mightn't have known herself until the last minute. She didn't let me know the last time either, when she arrived in the middle of the night. I can't say I knew she would come this time, but I felt and hoped she would: Joachim has his thirteenth birthday this month.

I saw her in the distance. I was up on the top balcony shaking out the *flokati* rugs when I noticed a bright blur coming up the road. She likes vivid colours, and that meant yet another score against her on the old women's tally sheet. She didn't go into mourning after her mother died but wandered around her garden wearing long shorts and shirt of a colour known in our youth as shocking pink. The locals were shocked, certainly, and murmured and tutted among themselves. Poor limited things: all they had to do was observe her step, which had become dragging and heavy, and her face, which was drawn and set with grief. There wasn't any light left in it at all. People here can only read the signs they are used to, are totally blind to any others.

The blur approached steadily and eventually sprang into focus. She was wearing her Akubra hat. Absolutely sure then, I rushed down the stairs to meet her. I paused, though, in the shadow of the high garden wall. Walls and outside doors are a part of peasant secretiveness: sheltered by both you can observe everything without being observed. She hadn't changed outwardly. Even in November it's sunny here; she was wearing a short-sleeved red shirt and the inevitable jeans and looked very much as she looked when I first met her all those years ago.

I squinted and saw emu feathers floating gently from the hatband. A symbol of endurance? A gesture of defiance? I also saw the flutter of at least one black headscarf as she passed. She's always been a good walker, and here she was again, swinging up the road, approaching in a set rhythm, head held high. I've seen her defeated; she's wept on my shoulder and confided in me many times, but such moments have always been very private ones. In public both of us hold our heads high even when we feel that every vertebra is cracking. 'Remember the Australian article of faith, Juliet,' she said once. 'Don't let the bastards get you down.' She's been unable to follow her own advice apparently.

I ran out into the road, calling her name. She stopped immediately and I saw then that she was very tired. She was, in more ways than one, simply putting one foot in front of the other. I burst into tears and flung myself on her, and there we stood in the pale sunlight, a tangle of arms and hat and luggage. 'Look at you,' I kept saying, and I don't know why, 'look at you'.

Hallo, Juliet,' she said quietly, as if with a great effort. 'I'm back. Where's Joachim?' Although she must have known he would be at school. She didn't say another word.

I helped her to her house, took her inside, made

her a cup of tea. She took her hat off and sat down. 'Welcome home,' I said, and immediately felt awkward and wished I hadn't. She looked at me silently and a tear slid down her cheek. Just the one. Still she said nothing.

That was ten days ago. She hasn't said much since.

I'll have to keep an eye on her, that seems obvious. It will do me good, will be like old times, and drag me away from my diary, which I've been spending too much time on lately. Am I becoming like her? Joanna's old enough now to help; she'll let me know how things are in the house and with Joachim's father. It's not clear how long this visit is to be. I haven't asked. Irene will tell me what she wants to tell me.

I had hoped she would come in this evening, in the same old way, but the same old ways don't last, are bound to die a natural death. I wish I had *not* said, 'Welcome home,' for in the moment that I saw that single tear roll down her cheek I knew I was looking at someone truly homeless, who is likely to remain so, even though she returns regularly to a solid, roofed pile of bricks and mortar.

Somewhere I've read that home is where language makes sense. It's not as simple as that though. Greek makes sense to me now – well, so it should, as I've been here such a long time and am not exactly stupid, even though I've felt very stupid very often in this place. But it can't ever make sense to me the way it makes sense to Pavlos, Joanna and Joachim. I accept that, but I don't know that Irene ever could. She wanted to make sense of Greeks and Greekness through language, but never succeeded. She's simply not a practical female.

What she is at present is an exhausted woman, a woman with a secret. I've an idea this secret has something to do with a place, a set of circumstances where not only language but everything else made sense. I suspect there was, at the very least, a flash of recognition, an unlooked-for and unexpected happiness which didn't last. Well, she might have known. At our age we need an inoculation against the disease of hope. She ought to know that it's pain that lasts, not happiness.

The gods are jealous creatures. It doesn't do to be happy, and brief, surprising happiness is the worst kind of all. She's a slow learner, a slow learner with an intractable memory. She remembers what she should forget: a time when things seemed simple, a time of certainty, of familiarity, rather than the constant infuriating difference that we have to put up with here. Most importantly, she remembers a cessation of pain. I'm almost certain that her pain was suspended for a short time. The voices of her childhood called, if I'm right, and she wanted to answer them.

I've forgotten lots of things because I've had to. I switch my head off. It's simple, once you get the hang of it. Irene's never learned the knack and probably won't now. A teacher who can't learn. I remember and tell myself what I've got: Pavlos, who loves me in his way, and Joanna, who loves me as children love their mothers. A beautiful house in a pretty place. A worthwhile job.

Irene will tell me what she wants to tell me, which means that I won't know, from day to day, whether she plans to stay or go. Whether she stays or not, it seems certain now that she'll always be a wanderer. She's wandered into the forest again and again, and what has she found as a result of all that restlessness? Quite possibly nothing, but still she persists. That's her nature: unable to compromise, unable to give up or give in. No wonder she's tired.

Perhaps I'll tell her what I want to tell her. And that is that the time has come, now that we're past our middle-age, to cut our losses, to call a halt to the search, for there's little more to be found. We can do all the searching we need to do here at home, for the human heart is always more intricate than any forest.

All we have, any of us, is the here, the now, the moment. It's futile to yearn for anything else, useless to look back and sigh for what is not. That's what I want to tell her. That's what I believe. Perhaps I *should* tell her. But I'm not sure. It might be a good idea to save myself both breath and effort. For she is, as I've said, a teacher who does not, will not, learn.

ALSO BY GILLIAN BOURAS

Aphrodite and the Others

Aphrodite – priest's wife, matriarch, illiterate – has lived in her village in the Peloponnese for eighty-six years. Her struggle and hardship have been echoed by national and international upheavals, by war, dictatorship and famine. In writing the story of her mother-in-law's life, Gillian Bouras recounts her own difficulties as an educated, independent Westerner coming to terms with a woman so culturally different and so domestically powerful.

But this book is much more than Aphrodite's story. It is a remarkable counterpoint of the oral tradition and the literate, the personal and the political, of individual voices murmuring against the clamour of wider events. Gillian Bouras, who moved from Australia to Greece in 1980, brings these two contrasting cultures into sharp relief. Taking up the themes of her earlier works, *A Foreign Wife* and *A Fair Exchange*, she weaves them into something which is at once factual and richly imaginative.

Winner, 1994 New South Wales State Literary Award.

ALSO BY GILLIAN BOURAS

A Fair Exchange

When Gillian Bouras, bestselling author of *A Foreign Wife*, went to live in a Greek village for a few months in 1980 she never imagined she would still be there ten years later. In *A Fair Exchange* she further explores the upheavals and pleasures of exchanging one home for another. Out of her experience has grown a love of words and the patterns they make in her life; and despite her nostalgia for Australia, she cannot resist the impact of foreign landscapes and the people that surround her.

ALSO BY GILLIAN BOURAS

A Foreign Wife

Gillian Bouras is an Australian married to a Greek. From the ambiguous position of a foreign wife, she writes of life in a Greek village. Her fellow villagers regard her, the migrant in their midst, as something of a curiosity. They, in turn, are the source of both her admiration and her perplexity.

In 1969 we bravely organised two weddings. An Orthodox ceremony was then a legal requirement of the Greek State, but I wanted some English spoken over me as well. The first service passed in a sort of blur ... A short time later I walked down a familiar fleur-de-lis carpet towards a Presbyterian minister who welded familiar words and music into a brief service of blessing. It was George's turn to be confused.